# The WHISPERLING TWINS

rlann Ráth Maonais
Rathmines Library
01-2228466

# HAYLEY HOSKINS

PUFFIN

PUFFIN BOOKS

UK | USA | Canada | Ireland | Australia
India | New Zealand | South Africa

Puffin Books is part of the Penguin Random House group of companies
whose addresses can be found at global.penguinrandomhouse.com.

www.penguin.co.uk
www.puffin.co.uk
www.ladybird.co.uk

First published 2024

001

Text copyright © Hayley Hoskins, 2024
Illustrations copyright © Kristina Kister, 2024

The moral right of the author and illustrator has been asserted

Set in 13/18pt Baskerville MT Std
Typeset by Jouve (UK), Milton Keynes
Printed and bound in Great Britain by Clays Ltd, Elcograf S.p.A.

The authorized representative in the EEA is Penguin Random House Ireland,
Morrison Chambers, 32 Nassau Street, Dublin D02 YH68

A CIP catalogue record for this book is available from the British Library

ISBN: 978–0–241–51452–8

All correspondence to:
Puffin Books
Penguin Random House Children's
One Embassy Gardens, 8 Viaduct Gardens, London SW11 7BW

MIX
Paper | Supporting
responsible forestry
FSC® C018179

Penguin Random House is committed to a
sustainable future for our business, our readers
and our planet. This book is made from Forest
Stewardship Council® certified paper.

*To Steve, for keeping me chipper and bringing me coffee <3*

*And to anyone who has ever felt a bit different or
'a bit much', this is for you — keep shining. x*

# PROLOGUE

## THE RIFT

### OAKDEAN-ON-SEVERN, 1917

The ghost waits patiently for the girls to notice him.

He can't quite remember how he got here, but he remembers *wishing* for something. *What was it?* He scrunches his face, trying to dredge the memory up from his brain. He was somewhere dark, that much he knows. Not one of those scary, *is there something under my bed?* sorts of dark. Somewhere . . . gentle. Safe. Like snuggling under the warmest, softest eiderdown on a frosty day with only your nose poking out.

And then he'd made his wish.

A roar of energy so powerful knocked any remaining breath from him and, in a blink, he is here. By the canal. Where bubbling laughter, splish-splashing water and the quiet thrum of turbines from the nearby docks slowly fill the space where his heart once beat. Narrowboats bob at the edge of the water, neat and gleaming with detailed paintwork. One has its name cleverly threaded through a spray of hot-pink flowers so lifelike the ghost swears he can smell their sweet scent.

The two girls must be ten years old, or thereabouts, younger than him by just a few summers. If he really tried, he could recall being their age. But there's too much pain in remembering, and so instead he's content just to watch them, smiling at their squeals of delight as they play catch. Ribbons stuffed into pinafore pockets, long, dark hair flying in their faces; their boots and stockings have been discarded on a grassy patch of ground where a large chestnut horse flicks away flies with her tail.

A small, brown dog yips and skitters up and down the towpath with every throw of the ball. 'No, Badger!' laughs one of the girls. 'It isn't for you! Your catch, Nin!'

The barge horse looks up from grazing and gently whinnies at the pup, her flanks shining like buffed conkers. *Conkers! I had a sixer one year, beast of a thing. Pals were all jealous. 'The Grand Destroyer' we called it* . . . The ghost laughs to himself, then realizes he can't remember any of his friends' names or their faces. A cloud of sadness rolls in.

But the gentle lift and fall of the moored boats is soothing. The ghost has always loved the water and his dark mood trickles away, as does the urge to speak to the girls. *Look at them. They're just happy little kids. Can't remember what I wanted to say, any road.*

And he doesn't want to interrupt their game. They're really good at it. No matter how extravagant, how daring each throw is, the catch is sure, always. They are connected, these children, like night and day, moon and tide. Sisters.

'Ten minutes, girls!' shouts a new voice. 'There's crumpets and jam for tea.' A smiling woman, hair swishing in her face, waves at the children from beyond the towpath. She shines, though only a little. Not everybody does. Just the special ones.

*What a lovely place*, thinks the ghost, looking admiringly at his surroundings: the water, the boats, the chocolate-box cottages. Over there, a friendly-looking pub, and a church and a tiny shop with fruit and vegetables displayed in stacked wicker baskets. *Did I live here? Before . . . ?*

Before what? He looks down at himself. Khaki trousers. Heavy hobnail boots, cloth bands wrapped from ankle to knee. *Puttees?* The word comes back to him in a flash, along with a memory of being knee-deep in mud. The smell of gun smoke. The thrum of fighter planes overhead. He puts his hands to his ears. *Make it stop. Please make it stop!*

The woman turns, as if tapped on the shoulder. She frowns and puts a hand to her throat.

*She's staring right at me.*

The girls stop their play.

'Oh, hello,' says one. She shines a little brighter than her sister. 'Where did you come from?'

'I made a wish,' he replies. 'But I can't remember what it was . . .' A tear rolls down his face.

But the girls aren't really listening. The one who said hello is pointing to something behind him. She stumbles to her sister's side, alarm scribbled between her brows. What does she see? The ghost looks back into the soft, gentle place he came from.

It is not as it was.

Darkness has crept in. The veil he somehow came through – the barrier between the living and the dead – pulls tight, like the stretched skin of a drum. Behind it he can see murky, crackling shadows and strange shapes that twist and jerk and squirm impatiently. An arm. A foot. A face. Pushing through the veil, into the living world. Pushing *towards* the girls.

And then the veil rips altogether.

The ghost stumbles backwards.

*The girls . . . I have to save them!*

He drags everything he has into this moment, pulling leaves and dirt and feathers and grit with him into a windstorm as he rushes forward desperately and roars: '*RUN!*'

The girls are already edging away from the shadows in panic, towards the water. The woman shouts at them to be careful; the small dog growls, baring his sharp little teeth.

The sisters reach for each other's hands.

The effect is instant: the world is ignited. Though they shone a little before, now – joined together – the girls blaze like a thousand sunrises. The ghost covers his eyes, dazzled.

There is a scream and a splash.

His arm drops to his side again; his eyes begin to clear. The last thing he sees as he starts to fade away are others like him, other ghosts pushing past the dark shadows, vying for the girls' attention. Not one or two, or even a dozen.

Thousands more soldiers, marching towards them.

## OAKDEAN-ON-SEVERN, LATE 1918

In front parlours all over the country, women are wondering if the men they love are still alive. Husbands, fathers, sons; bakers, accountants, schoolboys. Brave, hopeful men, cheerily waved off to war with flags and bunting and bread and dripping wrapped in brown paper. *The Great War*, they're calling it. I'm not so sure about that. Soldiers living in fear and filth, waiting to be shoved over the top of a trench, only to be mown down by machine guns on the orders of men with clean hands and shiny shoes?

Don't sound so great to me.

And still the women wait. Busying themselves,

knitting socks to send to their boys to *keep those feet warm*, like a well-turned heel is going to protect feet rotting from trench foot. Once the littlest kids are in bed and the day's chores are all done, when there's nothing left to fill the space where the bad thoughts leach in, the women check the calendar and count again the time since they last had word. *Seven months . . . how can it be?* Only then, when they can't bear the wait any longer, do they pull up the chairs, throw a black sheet over the table, and open the front door to someone who promises they can talk to the dead.

'*Is anybody there?*'

There may come a knock, or a scrape. Sometimes the woman will realize the noise came not from the spirit world but from the sneaky trickster she has invited into her parlour. Sometimes she won't.

And sometimes – rarely, for we're few in number – she'll be lucky and her guest will be someone genuine. A *real* whisperling. Like me.

'*Is anybody there?*'

That's the difference between the liars and the whisperlings. When we ask the question, the dead actually answer.

*

8

My name is Nin Esmond. Officially it's Violet, but no one calls me that. Me and my sister Lemon (officially it's Clemency, but no one calls *her* that, either) are whisperlings. Meaning we can talk to ghosts, to the dead.

It's written, although Mam can't show us exactly where, that we're to use our gift 'to help those left behind'. It is, Mam says, the 'whisperling way'. She *also* says that if my sister and I roll our eyes any harder they'll pop right out of our heads and then we'll be sorry.

We do our best to help, me and Lemon, but things are proper busy, ghost-wise. Most messages we get are for folk what live in the city, and it's a fair old plod from here up to Gloucester. There's no way we can get round 'em all. Instead, we hold group readings in the fusty, candle-lit snug of the canal-side pub where we live. *We*, being me, Lemon, the mams (our mam, Rose, and her partner, Bessie) and Badger, the best dog in the world.

It's been a lot to get used to.

'Have you started your lady time?' asked Bessie, boldly, when we first realized something about me was different. I nodded, a blush burning my cheeks. Bessie is so *modern*. 'It's likely, then, that that's brought on your gifts. A bit of a soaking in the canal wouldn't cause your powers to grow overnight.'

She was teasing, but it was too soon for it, and besides, she's not a whisperling. What would she know?

'I *died*, Bessie!'

'Only for a minute. Don't be so dramatic.'

I sighed. Bessie is not one for indulging you.

But . . .

That minute made my whisperling abilities extra sensitive.

That minute made me extra visible to ghosts.

That minute was long enough for me to take a step through the door between this life and the next, and not quite long enough to close it behind me again.

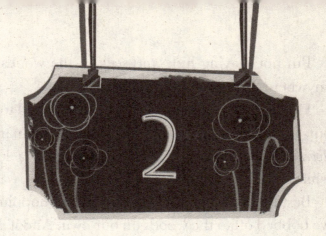

2

'Together forever?' I uncross my legs and stretch one over the narrow gap between our beds to nudge my sister's toes. She ignores me. 'Lemon?'

'No.' She flicks my foot away. 'I don't want to play.'

Pouting, I tuck my leg back under me. 'Just a quick game?'

'What, in here?'

She has a point – our room *is* tiny – but still, something deflates inside me. I lean against the wall with its coat of rough plaster like a layer of fork-peaked cream on top of a trifle. My stomach growls. Stupid rationing.

'We could go to the copse?' I suggest. 'Like we used to.'

'I'm not playing hide-and-seek in the woods or anywhere, Nin. We're not babies.'

'I know that. It's just . . . oh, *forget it*.' It used to be our favourite game, with its own special name. *Together forever*. But we haven't played it in a long while.

'Besides,' says Lemon, 'the mams'd be hoppin' if we bobbed off to the woods on our own. And if I'm going to do something to get in trouble, I might as well go visit Ivy.'

Ivy is Lemon's friend. She's fun and pretty and clever and used to live in *London*, until a bomb landed on her primary school. She's often unwell, on account of having shrapnel still stuck in her innards, which makes her even more fascinating. Lemon hangs on her every word.

I hate Ivy.

Lemon nudges me back with her foot, by way of apology. 'What you writing? More of them poems?' She nods at the notebook and pencil next to me. 'Or you practisin' your entry for the grand old Book of Devona, if we ever get it back.'

'Shh!' I warn, glancing at the door. 'Mam'll skin you if she hears you talking like that!'

'What?' says Lemon at a bold volume. 'It's not

my fault she was given some precious relic to look after and it got pinched, is it?'

'Lemon . . .'

It was years ago, but Mam goes on and on about losing that book as if it is the worst thing ever to have happened. *It is not*, she says, *a laughing matter*.

'Oh, come on,' my sister teases, eyes glittering with mischief. 'It's just an old book with boring old stories written by creepy old people. Whoever nicked it probably chucked it in the canal or used it to wipe their bum.'

'LEMON!'

'Talking of boring old stories —'

'Hey!' I grab for my notebook but I'm not quick enough and Lemon whips it away, laughing, spinning like a top around the bedroom. 'Give it BACK!' I spring up and lunge for her but she darts backwards, bouncing from one foot to the other like she's playing hopscotch.

'What?' she says, jumping on to her bed. 'And miss out on wonders such as this?' She holds the book up so my swiping arms can't reach her and theatrically clears her throat. 'Silence, please!' she says, doing her best posh voice like we hear on the newsreels. 'Ay am de-*layted* to share with you the latest, glorious wahrk by Miss Nin Esmond –' she winks at me – 'spinster of this parish –'

'Oi!' I yell, but I'm laughing now too. She's such an idiot. *Please, just not the one about the water. I can't bear –*

'Ahem, yes, a groundbreaking wahrk, entitled "Ghosts as Water".'

I drop to my knees and put my head in my hands. '*Nooo,*' I groan. A paw touches my leg and I lift the covers to see Badger, our little brown dog, stretched out underneath. 'Don't listen, old fella,' I whisper. 'I'm not,' and I clamp the eiderdown over my ears.

There's a knock at the door. 'What are you two nobbagawnies up to now?'

The mattress springs bounce like pistons as Lemon jiggles delightedly. 'Bessie!' she shrieks. 'Quick!'

'No, no, NO!' But it's too late; the door creaks open and Bessie pads into the room. I don't even need to see her to know she's got her arms crossed and a grin plastered over her face. 'Clemency! That's enough,' scolds Bessie, but there's a giggle in her voice. 'Your mam has got a bit of a headache, so behave yourselves.'

Something lands on my head with a *phlump*. I reach for it. 'Hey, that's my pillow!' I yell at Bessie, but she's already gone.

'Well then, what about this one?' Lemon clears her throat. '*They surround us —*'

'The Righteous,' I squeak in response.

'*They are the breeze that brushes your cheek . . . They are in the empty chair.*'

I don't know where it came from originally, but we've scared each other with this odd little verse about these faceless bogeymen ever since we could speak.

I join in with my deepest monster voice. '*They are . . .*'

Lemon whips the bedcovers up and shouts in my face, '*UNDER YOUR BED!*' and I scream, squeeze my eyes shut and blindly grab at the covers to pull them back over me.

'Stop that at once!'

Mam's voice cuts through the fun like a pin to a rubber balloon. I lift the eiderdown from my head.

'Sorry, Mam.'

'I've told you both before: The Righteous are real, they're dangerous to whisperlings, and their hateful jealousy isn't a thing to be mocked. And I understand how little the Book of Devona means to you both, given you were so young when it was taken, but it's not a joke – none of it is.' Mam shakes her head. 'I hope they never become more than a silly poem to you, I really do.'

We wait until we hear her footsteps padding back down the stairs.

'It's not a poem, it doesn't even blimmin' rhyme,' mutters Lemon, and we both snort with laughter into our pillows so Mam doesn't hear us.

3

It's the middle of the night and there's a ghost in our kitchen.

She's there when I come down for a glass of water, sitting at the kitchen table as if she's about to take tea. 'Hello,' I say, the odd prickle in my neck now making sense. There's a tiny shift in the air as the night exhales, making room for her.

She's clouded in mist, like shimmering steam from a magic kettle. 'Is it you?' she asks, peering at me from dark-lashed eyes. Her skin is milky-pale, and she's dressed in her Sunday best. In the old days, folk used to take photographs of those who had died. They'd be wearing something like this. Posed like puppets with open eyes painted on their closed lids. One last memory for those left behind.

'No,' I say. It's Lemon she wants; this is *her* friend, after all. I turn back to the stairs, meaning to wake my sister, but the girl is now in front of me, palm flat to my chest. I look down . . . The covered buttons of my nightgown are visible through her hand, the shape of the staircase hovering behind her. I slowly look back up at her face.

'What happened, Ivy?'

She doesn't have long; the light surrounding her will carry on warming until it's as golden as sunrise. We whisperlings call this moment *the burn*, when the soul leaves the body and passes on to whatever's beyond.

'Mamma said not to worry,' she replies. 'It's just a bit of bomb dust making my tummy hurt.' She taps at her belly.

'She's probably right,' I say, humouring her. Tears prick at the back of my eyes.

'*Ninny*,' she says with a musical giggle. I bite my lip. I *hate* being called that. 'Don't cry. I know I'm dead.' Her face falls. 'But I can bear it, really I can.' She looks behind her. 'It's just . . .' She stops herself, and puts a translucent hand to her mouth.

'I know,' I say. 'You want to speak to Lemon.' I lean to one side, so as not to shout straight at her.

'Lemon! Lemon, get down here!' When I glance back, the glow that surrounds Ivy is too bright to look at directly.

'Tell Lem I'll miss her,' she says, just as I hear my sister lumbering out of bed.

But it's too late. By the time Lemon has reached the kitchen, the burn has taken her friend, and for the next few weeks she can barely look at me.

4

Sometime later, after Ivy's funeral, there is a thaw between my sister and me. We're friends again, just about.

'Look, Ninny.' Lemon shoves a newspaper in my face, jabbing a finger at an article at the bottom of the page.

*Ninny.* I knew it would cheer her that ghostly Ivy had called me that, but I'm beginning to regret telling her. I pull my head back and lift my glasses. 'What am I looking at?'

Her finger hovers next to an advert for Lifebuoy soap and a public health message that says *Washing hands saves lives*. I shudder. While we're spared death by bullets and bayonets, the flu could creep under our door at any minute. Even school is shut to stop the spread, which is a terrible thing that is very difficult not to be pleased about.

**Missing Girl Believed To Be in Gloucester:**
Maeve McQueen is described as having long, red hair and a pale, freckled complexion. A source states that she's 'probably one of them creepers' and is 'likely up to high jinks'.

'Creepers?' The word is an old-fashioned, hateful term for 'whisperlings'. Even the sneeriest of folk tend not to use it – at least, not in public. Why do people have to be so mean?

'And what is *this*?'

'Fairies, Nin. Haven't you heard? They're all the rage.'

Alongside the newspaper's spiteful words about poor Maeve McQueen, there's a charming piece about two young girls taking photographs of *fairies*, who they say live at the bottom of their garden.

'Unbelievable!' I peer at a photograph of a young girl surrounded by tiny, dancing creatures with butterfly-like wings. 'Is this real? It can't be real, can – *Ow*, that hurt!' I rub at my cheek where Lemon flicked it.

My sister looks at me like I've put my shoes on my ears. 'It's bogging *fairies*, Nin, what do you think? They'd rather everyone was talking about *them* than any missing whisperlings. It's a smokescreen!'

I scan the rest of the paper. With news of more losses at the front, I can see why fairies might be a welcome distraction. 'We don't know the missing girls are whisperlings, not for sure.'

'Yeah, well, Mam's letters from her whisperling friends mentioned missing girls in their town as well.'

I sit up. 'What letters?' Lemon is *such* a snooper!

She dismisses me with a wave of a hand. My chest tightens. Lemon's thirst for adventure is tinder-dry after years living under the threats of The Righteous, the war, and now the poxy Spanish flu. We are both bored, but Lemon especially. If anything sparks that touchpaper, she'll spin off like a Catherine wheel and I'll burn my fingers trying to catch her.

'Well, we can't just go running off to investigate, can we?' I add. 'We're only young girls ourselves . . . it wouldn't be safe.' I expect Lemon to throw a pillow at my head, but she doesn't. She sits, thoughtfully tapping her bottom lip with a finger.

'Safe?' she says, quietly. 'No one's *safe*. Look at Ivy: her parents moved out of London to protect her and what good did it do?'

I don't know what to say, and silence blankets our bedroom like newly fallen snow. Lemon gives the tiniest shrug and purses her lips. She won't look at me. Can't look at me.

*Tell me*, I will her. *Tell me what you've been doing when you get up in the middle of the night and sneak off to who knows where. Is it because of Ivy? Are you sad? Please tell me. Let me help.*

And then a shout from Mam breaks the spell. Lemon slides to the floor like an eel and reaches under her bed for the dressing-up suitcase. 'I'm sure we'll think of something,' she says brightly, 'but there's no time for it now. We've got a messaging to get ready for.'

5

The dead creep in like the shallow wash of low tide.

There's always movement in The Bargeman's; it's one of the oldest pubs in the county. Candles squished into jam jars throw flickering shadows against the rough plaster. I dare a look. But not all of these shadows are cast by wax and wick and – *Oh my!* My breath catches – What was *that*? A shape slips from the –

'Oi! Back in the room, drippy-knickers!' Lemon spins past me, clicking her fingers in my face like castanets, heels hammering like a flamenco dancer. She pauses, red-faced and wheezing, raises a finger to show she needs to catch her breath, and then she's off again, heels striking the ground so fast I half expect them to spark. '*Wheeeee!*' I clamp my hands to my ears to drown her out and peer at her through my curtain of hair. She's stopped dancing to tug at the bodice of her dress: a too-big, ink-black, Victorian-era gown with poufy sleeves and ruffles that tickle your neck – at least, it did the one time I tried it on. She thinks she looks *great*, but she looks stupid and I'm *glad* she got her mitts on it first, so there.

'She's only trying to cheer you up,' says Gran quietly. 'You know how jittery you get before a messaging.' She settles beside me, her fuzzy hair clouding like dandelion fluff under a white mob cap. Her face is the shape of a cottage loaf, dimples poked there by fingers checking to see if she's proved. 'I know she's a bit of a show-off. Your mam was the same at her age.' She rummages in her pinny pocket and pulls out a boiled sweet, gleefully brandishing it like a magician pulling silk scarves from a sleeve. 'Want one?'

I shake my head. Fine, Lemon's just trying to help, but she still does my nut in. I wince as she knocks into a table, almost upending a pint glass. It's steadied, mid-topple, by a wiry-looking lad with shaking fingers. He says something to my sister I can't catch. Lemon sees me looking. She freezes like a statue, then widens her eyes and pulls a comically horrified face, like that famous painting of someone screaming. I shake my head. One cheek dimples disloyally and straight away my sister twirls over to me, grinning like a loon. 'You're such a spanner,' I say.

'Oh, shush. I am an artiste!' she declares, flicking her hair over her shoulder. It's waist length, poker straight and the colour of a raven's wing, just like mine. She always wears a yellow silk scarf, usually to fasten it in a plait; tonight it's wrapped round her head and tied under one ear, loose ends flowing over her shoulder. 'Someone's got to be the star of the show!' says Lemon with a shimmy. 'If you want to do the messaging by yourself, be my guest.' She turns her head away with a theatrical sniff.

I know she's kidding, but the thought of everyone's eyes on me and me alone makes me want to gip. I worry at a loose thread on the seam of my black glove, wiggling it with a finger like a wobbly tooth, breathing in and out slowly to try and distract myself. But it's too late, and my gaze wanders over to the thick, rippled glass of the pub windows and the canal beyond.

*The water.*

I close my eyes and I'm back there, at the water's edge. I feel it all at once, in pin-sharp detail: my foot slipping, the rush of embarrassment, and a hoot of laughter from my sister when I splash backwards; the whip-crack of cold when I hit the water, the water weeds that grab at my legs – *they're tightening, I can't get free!* – the pulse of terror and pain as the canal's filthy water rushes into my mouth and I'm kicking, kicking, lungs burning, *don't breathe the water in, don't breathe in, don't . . . breathe . . . Am I breathing?* And then . . . nothing. Just me, the dark, and what looked like a thousand glittering diamonds . . .

'– Nin?' My sister speaks from a place that sounds far away. 'Nin, it's all right, I'm here,' she says, positioning herself deliberately between me and my view of the water. I open my eyes and affection plunges into my tummy like a big, fat bird swooping on to a perch. She cups my face in her hands and wipes my tears away with her thumbs. 'One day the war will be over, things will go back to normal and there'll be no more messagings. You won't have to be afraid of all these ghosts, or the water, or anything.'

I admire her optimism.

'And the mams'll stop worrying about the stupid Self-righteous or whatever they're called, and we'll be free to have fun again!'

'*The* Righteous,' I mutter through squished cheeks, unable to let her go uncorrected even though I know she's joking. Lemon leans forward to touch my forehead with hers. A spark passes between us.

'Ogethertay oreverfay?' she whispers in our code.
*Together forever.*

'Oreverfay ogethertay,' I reply.
*Forever together.*

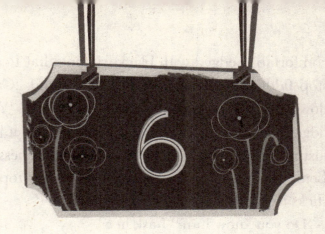

The snug is *full* of girls and women. Before the war, this would have been out of the question. 'You're going to a public house, Hilda? Alone? Without a man? Hold my Horlicks, for I've a swoon approaching.' But the war has punctured men-shaped holes in everything, and women have filled the gaps. In factories, in offices. Down the pub. Some folk don't like it. The mams say there's those who prefer women to 'know their place'. Which is *where*, exactly? *Wherever we want to be*, says Mam, *and we won't be told that we 'can't' or 'shouldn't'*. They say there's even talk, finally, of women getting the vote. I didn't know we *couldn't* vote. What kind of bobbins rule is that?

Lemon and I sit together on a velvet-covered curly-legged piano stool. The seat is threadbare but comfortable, edged with black fringing that I can't stop fiddling with. Lemon flicks my hand. 'Calm down,' she says from the side of her mouth. 'Your fidgetin' is makin' the piano keys tinkle.' But it isn't just me. There are red splodges of nervousness on Lemon's cheeks, and when she smiles her top lip sticks to her teeth.

'Do you know him?' I ask her.

'Who?'

'Him.' Beyond the snug, the boy staggers back into the bar from taking a wee in the canal. 'The one whose pint you spilled.' Not that it was *his* beer; he hasn't bought one drink all night, the cheapskate. I should've told Mam or Bessie what he was doing, scavenging anything left unfinished, but when the soldiers came in earlier I thought he'd gone. He reappeared just in time to chug *their* leftover dregs before Mam cleared the glasses away.

The boy see-saws on long, spindly legs. Little wonder he's unsteady. It was whiskies all round for the Glorious Glosters, who were toasting an injured young infantryman in a wheelchair. The Gloucestershire Regiment is their official title but no one calls them that, least not round here. 'By our deeds we are known!' they'd said in unison, clinking their glasses. I couldn't look at the young man's legs, or the space where they'd once been: trousers neatly folded and pinned just above his knees.

'At least he's alive,' said Gran, which is hard to argue with.

*By our deeds we are known.* I like that.

Lemon takes a sip of water and runs her tongue over her gums. 'Good evening, everyone,' she begins. 'Thank you for coming. As ever, we can't guarantee if any ghosts will come to speak to us. But if you recognize who a message may be for, please let Bessie know.' Lemon gestures towards Bessie, who sits at the back, poised like a reporter with her notepad and pencil. Her hair is long and plaited and she wears it looped and coiled like a snake, tied at the nape of her neck with a scarf of emerald green.

Lemon shuffles on the seat towards me, pushes a stray hair back under her yellow headscarf and holds out her hands. 'Ready?'

I nod, although I'm not ready, not really, but still I remove my gloves and shove them under my leg. I close my eyes and place my hands in hers.

*Whoosh!*

Something swooshes around my body like a magical paintbrush. It starts at my fingers, runs up my arms, around my head then back down again, sparking through my hands into my sister's, where it does the same to her, around and around and around, binding us together in a ribbon of light. Lemon grips my hands tighter, fingernails digging into my palms as the air around us crackles and shifts.

*It's happening.* I open my eyes.

They can see us now, the ghosts, and they can speak to us, too, if they like. A shiver of something catches my eye, peeling from the walls, sliding around us like oil blackened in a pan . . .

I blink, hard. Odd, scattered shapes swim into my vision: a widening cavernous, black mouth; the scratchy point of a witch's hat; a strange, trembling garland of paper dolls. I shake them away, not understanding what they mean, and also not wanting any of the images to linger. Seeing ghosts is one thing, but this is proper creepy.

Lemon and I exchange a look and then the lights go out.

7

Turns out we were gone from the real world for yonks.

'What happened?' I ask. 'Where is everyone?'

Mam sits next to us on a chair that wasn't there when we started. 'It's nothing to worry about,' she says, but she won't meet my eye. 'We asked everyone to leave, that's all.' Save a couple of stragglers at the bar, the pub is empty.

'Why?' asks Lemon. 'Didn't we make contact with anyone?' She looks at me, confused. 'I'm sure we did.'

This isn't unusual – our memories can often be a bit fuzzy after a messaging, but something definitely feels off.

'Lemon's right,' I say. 'We definitely did. Mam, tell us, please.'

'Well, you had three or four messages, two of which were for someone here.' Hearing this, I have a vague memory of a woman and a baby. 'And Bessie made a note of the others. We think they're for the lad at the butcher's shop in the next village. The ghost said his name was –'

'Mam!' snaps Lemon. 'This is normal stuff! What *happened*?'

'Nothing! It was nothing.' Mam smooths her skirts and stands up, muttering something about tidying up. She moves swiftly from table to table, gathering glasses as if we're not here, while Lemon simmers next to me, ready to boil over.

There is a clatter, followed by a noise like a sack of rubbish being dragged over stones. 'We're closed!' shouts Bessie from the main part of the pub. 'Hey! Watch it!'

It's the lad from earlier, staggering towards us like his legs are made of wet string. Bessie's behind him, brandishing a broom like a bayonet. Fumes belch from his mouth like from a drunken dragon; he must've polished off *everything* the soldiers left behind.

'I thought you said you could do this!' he slurs. 'Where was he then? Where's my message? You're a liar!' His face is an inch from Lemon's and she scrunches her eyes shut and turns away.

'Ow! That hurt!' The boy rubs at his side and tries to grab Bessie's broom handle, but she's too quick and twirls away from him like a drum majorette.

'I told you, we're *closed*,' she repeats, tapping the palm of her hand with the end of the broom. Don't make me poke you again.'

'That's enough!' Mam steps between them, her arms full of glasses. She blows back her fringe. 'That's enough,' she says, more quietly this time. 'Thank you, Bessie. I'm sure he doesn't want any trouble.' She turns to my sister. 'You all right, Clemency?'

'Get outta my way, lady! I got no argument with you.' The boy puts a hand on Mam's shoulder, pushing her aside.

Gran whooshes forward, shoving him back. 'You leave my great-granddaughter be!' she shrieks.

The boy stumbles, sweeping his hands over his body as if to rid himself of fleas. 'Wh-what was that?'

Mam weaves her way to the bar, where she deposits the glasses with a clatter, then rolls up her sleeves and turns round to face him. 'Now, my lad, you have no argument with *anyone* here.' She cocks her head to one side, perhaps weighing up whether she could carry him to the canal to dunk his head in the water, as she and Bessie do with many a drunk. 'So pack it in. You are frightening my girls and I'll not have it.' Her hair flops in her face and she shoves it behind her ear with an irritable grimace.

'I knew you creepers were full of it. You're all talk!'

Mam steps forward and folds her arms. 'You come into my pub, into my *home*, and make an unholy scene for *talk*? And using that nasty, old-fashioned word for us as well. Shame on you. That's no way for a young man —' she tips her head – 'a young *soldier* to conduct himself.'

'I'm no soldier . . . Wh-who told you I were?' His eyes dart round the pub. 'D'you know me?'

'I don't know your name,' says Mam. 'But I can see you're upset.' She nods at his jacket. 'And I can see your regimental badge.'

He slaps a hand over his pocket. He must have stolen that badge. Maybe one of the Glosters dropped it.

I peer at him. He can't be a soldier – he's far too young. Apart from a red scarf tied round his neck, he is largely colourless. His hair is sandy, short at the neck and sides but with the top left scruffy and jagged, as if the razor was abandoned mid-cut for a knife and fork. He catches me looking.

'Wha's you guiling at?' he slurs. He's very drunk indeed and points a finger at me, then spins round to point at Lemon. 'Hey! Woo, what the . . . ?'

'Look,' Mam tries again. 'I'm sorry you didn't get your message, but it doesn't work like that. It isn't up to us which ghosts decide to come by. Anyone who says they can do that is having you on, and that would be cruel.' The lad deflates like a schoolboy who's just had his catapult confiscated.

'I wish it were possible,' Mam continues, her tone softer, and she puts a hand on his arm. Then she places her other hand on his back and slowly, very slowly, walks him towards the door. 'I'd contact Great Uncle Harry and find out what he did with the family silver. Or I'd ask Queen Victoria if she's reunited with her precious Prince Albert. *Or*,' she continues, jaw clenched, 'I'd ask if anyone knew who'd stolen our precious book and whether they'd mind scaring the bejesus out of them to get it back.'

37

She takes a breath, and Lemon and I roll our eyes at the mention of that bleedin' book. 'But you can't *force* a particular spirit to make contact. They'll come through if they see the whisperling glow and if they want to, but that's all. And yes, it's true that my girls are especially shiny.' She smiles over at me. 'Which is why we've felt duty-bound to do these messagings. We just want to do our bit, to give people the chance to say their goodbyes, if they can. That's all it is. I'm sorry you didn't get your message, I really am.' She stands outside the door with him, looking at him kindly.

'I'm sorry, Missus Pub Lady.' His eyes are glassy and he scrubs at them with the back of his sleeve. 'I miss 'im, tha's all.'

The poor lad.

Gran, satisfied now that things are under control, dusts her hands together and disappears through the wall, leaving behind a puff of talcum and the faint sickly scent of boiled sweets. I smile to myself. At least there are *some* upsides to seeing all these ghosts.

'Grief is the price we pay for love, young man,' says Bessie, who joins them by the door with a piece of cold pie she's fetched from the larder. She shoves it into the boy's pocket. 'Now, be off home with you.'

'Home?' He stops. 'And where might *home* be, for me?' He turns, snarling once again at Lemon. 'You said you could do it!' He shakes his fist at her. 'You're just like them other fakers! An' what the bleedin' hell was all that screaming for?' he shouts, taking another step into the pub towards her, but the next instant a couple of burly pub regulars have grabbed an arm each and bundled him back out of the door. He staggers away along the towpath, making rude hand gestures to the men who threw him out, and then doubles over to vomit, just missing his boots.

Lemon and I look at each other in horror.

*Who was screaming?*

Mam pours two cups of coffee from a silver pot and places one in front of Bessie. The smell of roasted beans fills the tiny kitchen and Mam cradles her cup, warming her hands. She blows gently, the steam dancing around her head like a fading phantom. There's such a throbbing in my temples, and I'm amazed Lemon hasn't yet exploded like a volcano.

'What did that boy mean? What screaming?' she asks.

'He was talking nonsense, love,' Bessie says. 'You saw him, he was as drunk as a lord!' She laughs unconvincingly.

'It's nothing to worry about,' adds Mam.

'I don't believe either of you,' says Lemon, flatly. She's tired, as we both are after a messaging. Her thumb finds her mouth like it used to when she was a baby, and she leans her head on Bessie's shoulder.

'I think it's time, girls, especially after that boy's performance . . .' Mam trails off, shaking her head. Her hair falls over her eye but she doesn't bother to tuck it behind her ear. 'Tonight's messaging was the last one for a good long while. Perhaps forever.'

Lemon opens her mouth to protest, but Mam raises a finger to silence her. 'Please, love, not now. It feels like ever since the book was stolen –' Mam grabs a tea-towel and flicks it at me like she's cracking a whip. I hadn't meant to groan out loud. Even Lemon looks at me in surprise. 'I understand you're tired of that story, Nin. It was so long ago you can barely remember it. But it's true: since it was stolen everything has gone wrong. The war, then the rift and your accident, the awful flu. And yes, the missing girls, too.' Lemon and I exchange a glance at Mam's acknowledgement. 'But I don't have the energy tonight. To argue about any of it.'

'But –'

'No, Lemon.' Mam rubs her temples. 'And it's best you two don't go anywhere without us for a while, until we try and work this all out.'

'What?' Lemon is on her feet. 'That's not fair! We barely go outside anyway, and never further than the village! We're safe enough in Oakdean, surely . . . People know us and –'

'People may know us, Clemency, but there was enough chatter after tonight's messaging to suggest they may not all care if you went missing too.'

9

As a canal-side pub we offer stabling for barge horses overnight, a break before their work recommences at the light of day. There's no need to groom them before they sleep, but me and Lemon like to. There's something comforting about the feel of your hand under a brush-strap and the warm flank of a chestnut cob against your cheek.

I lay out some hay, filling in some small, flattened patches (maybe Badger has been sleeping in here), and scoop fresh water from the butt to fill the drinking troughs. It's been days since the last messaging and we're all still off balance, as if a big giant has lifted up the pub, twisted it round and dropped it back down again, only this time just off its foundations. I try and remember the images that swam in front of my eyes but I can't. And when I question Mam about the scream, she plays it down, obviously regretful she said anything at all.

'Can you pass me that?' I ask Lemon, gesturing at a rake propped against the wall.

She looks at it – it's right next to her, leaning at a similar angle to her – and back at me. She reaches into her pinafore pocket, brings out a crust of bread and takes a huge bite, licking her lips and deliberately chewing as slack-jawed as a cow. 'Don't tell me what to do,' she says, looking me up and down. 'You're always telling me what to do.'

'I *asked* you to pass me the rake, I didn't tell you what to do with it.' I glare at her. 'Although I do have a few suggestions.' *Shove it up your bum*, maybe. And it wouldn't have killed her to bring me a snack too.

Lemon steps over the rake, curling a lock of hair round her finger as she paces distractedly around the stables, pausing by one of the horses to stroke its velvety nose. 'There, there, Nutty. You'd run free if you could, wouldn't you? Shake off that bridle and –'

'Oh, for heaven's SAKE!' I sputter so much I can barely get the words out. 'You're as subtle as a brick! No, Nutty would *not* shake off 'er bridle and run free; she's very comfortable here, thank you very much, aren't you, old girl?' Nutty flicks her head in agreement. I narrow my eyes at my sister. 'I know you're up to something, Lemon. If the mams get wind of yer plotting, they'll not let you leave this place until you're dead, you mark my words.'

'I'm not plotting *anything*,' she replies, eyes wider than saucers. 'So *please* stop bossing me ABOUT!' She yells the last word, suspiciously outraged.

I flinch, glancing back towards the kitchen. 'Shush yer big neck! The mams'll be out!'

'And how are they going to punish us? Send us off to the front?' Lemon pulls a lock of black hair across her face, scrunching up her mouth to hold it in place below her nose like a moustache. '*Your country needs YOU!*' she says, pointing a finger at me just as Lord Kitchener does in the army recruitment poster.

'Uncanny,' I say, reluctantly smiling.

We say goodnight to the horses – only two tonight, a pretty piebald called Pippin, and Nutty, who is ours, taken in when her boatman owner went off to war. She'd have been rounded up and taken to the front with the other horses in the village, but being old and slightly lame, she escaped that fate, which was lucky for us.

'Those missing girls, though,' whispers Lemon. 'I can't do nothing about it, Nin.'

I tighten up. 'Of course you can do nothing! It's so easy doing nothing – I do it all the time! Anyway, what do you think you could actually do?'

Lemon presses her lips together so tightly they lose colour, trapping her answer inside her.

A burst of something formless and screaming pops into my head – the same vision I had at the messaging. I shake it away. 'Please, Lemon. The mams are right: it's dangerous out there.'

'Yes, well, you're frightened of everything, aren't you?' Lemon squashes her voice down, trying to be quiet. Her eyes are wild, and remind me of Nutty's that time we all saw an off-course German zeppelin drop so low over the canal we swore we could see the colour of the pilot's cap. 'Whisperlings stick together, Nin. It's the number-one rule.'

I glare at her over my glasses, angry now. 'You've never even *met* another whisperling, and all of a sudden you're some sort of expert? All this "whisperlings sticking together" nonsense,' I continue. 'It's fairy tales! Like that stupid book.'

'What?' It's as if I've slapped her. 'The Book of Devona?'

'Yes, the Book of Devona.' I pull a face at her, like we do when we're being cheeky behind the mams' backs. 'I'm glad it was stolen. Even the name of it annoys me, it's so pompous.'

'You don't mean that!'

'Oh, so it's all right for *you* to call it "boring old stories written by creepy old people", but if *I* dare say anything bad about it, you get yer knickers in a knot.'

We joke about the book because it's easier than admitting the truth. The Book of Devona is the whisperlings' bible, passed down through generations, sharing stories and wisdom, and threading an almost magical connection through us all. 'It's for those that come after,' Mam had explained. She'd told us some things from it – annoyingly, that 'whisperlings stick together' being one of them – and although very young, Nin and I were about to start studying it properly just before it was stolen. 'Knowledge is power,' Mam says. She was devastated, having been trusted to look after it while Great Aunt Peggy, its usual keeper, was overseas. The theft caused an outcry in the whisperling world but in the meantime war broke out, which has hindered the search. I don't mean to be snippy about it. Lemon's right – I'm just scared.

'Those missing girls may not even be whisperlings,' I mutter.

'So? Does that make them less important?'

'Of course not!' I walked straight into that one. 'But what exactly do you think you can do?'

'I DON'T KNOW!' she yells. 'Just . . . something! We're whisperlings, Nin! Surely we can –'

'Oh, for heaven's, sake!' I snap, losing patience. 'You know, you really *are* a bit much!'

It's a mean line, and I regret it immediately. Tears prick at my eyes. I don't know why I said it. It's spiteful and untrue. My sister is one hundred per cent herself, and I'm sorr–

*Oof!* I stagger back. 'You . . . you *pushed* me!'

'Maybe it's not that *I'm* too much, Nin.' She pauses, dragging in breath to deliver a fiery blow. 'Maybe *you*'re just not enough!'

I can't stop myself either. 'You know, Lemon . . .' The words in my head are building to a terrible pressure – 'You go on about *our* gift and *our* powers, but it isn't really like that, is it? It isn't really *ours*, is it?'

48

'Shut up,' she says.

'I will not! It's mine, isn't it? *My* gift. I'm the one that sees the ghosts, I'm the one they seek out. Yer only use is yer big mouth.'

'Take. That. Back.' Lemon's nose almost touches mine. I can see hazel flecks in her blue-grey eyes, breathe in the tang of carbolic from our earlier bath, and a waft of floral: Mam's perfume, which my sister dabs behind her ears for courage.

'No. Not in front of the horses,' I say, ridiculously, as the Lemon storm rolls in and – *whomp* – I'm on the floor, mouth filled with horse bedding. 'Gran!' I shriek, and she's there in an instant, whirring the hay up like tumbleweed as Lemon skitters back until she's pressed against the stable wall.

'Please, girls, no good will come of this,' says Gran, holding a hand out to each of us.

'Wh-what's she saying?' Lemon squints, trying to see Gran, but she can't, she can't! It might be *years* before her powers are strong enough!

'She's saying you should know yer place,' I lie.

'Violet!' Gran's ghost scolds me, whipping up a sheaf of straw and throwing it in my direction. 'That's very unkind.' She goes to my sister's side and pats her arm to be comforting.

'Where is she? Is Gran still here?'

I pause for a moment. I'm being an absolute brat. 'No,' I say, decisively. 'She's gone. You probably bored 'er to death, again.'

'It's not my fault I can't see her. There's no need to be a cow.'

'And it isn't my fault I *can*. It isn't my fault I'm a *better* whisperling than you,' I finish, triumphant, ignoring the tear rolling down my sister's cheek. 'You couldn't even see the ghost of yer so-called best friend Ivy. So, Lemon, exactly what use *are* you?'

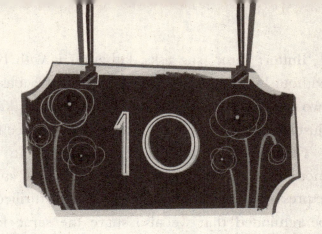

'Supper's ready!' shouts Mam from the kitchen. 'Come on, girls, it's late!'

It's almost ten but it's been an unusual evening and this is Mam's way of settling things before bedtime. Bessie has already gone up; she's singing a daft little song about a drunken sailor and her expressive lilt is comforting through the walls of the old building. A waft of toasted bread hits my nose but, instead of my mouth watering, I'm nauseous.

In the warmth of the kitchen the valve on my steaming temper releases little by little. A fork rests on the grate with a large slab of bread on its prongs. Mam wraps a striped tea-towel round her hand, lifts the fork and plops the golden, fragrant toast on to a plate on the kitchen table.

'Butter? Jam?' she asks, lathering it with both without listening for a reply. She cuts the toast in two equal halves, hesitating as she lifts the knife. 'Just like my girls,' she says, eyes flicking between us.

Tears prick at the back of my eyes. In this moment, Lemon and I share the same sullen expression and, as ever, neither of us is thrilled to be reminded that we also share the same face. Lemon was born first, by seventeen minutes. You would think it was seventeen years. 'I'm the oldest,' she would say, practically from the moment she could speak. Always, in her head, entitled to the bigger slice of cake, the first read of a book, the first play with a toy. It's only natural, therefore, that she would expect to have the lion's share of this stupid whisperling gift. My heart hardens. She's *jealous*. For once, it's me who's special.

Sometimes these days it feels as though we are barely related, let alone twins – and identical ones, at that. It was not always so. We still mirror each other in many, unbreakable ways. She is left-handed, I am right. She has a birthmark in the shape of a half-moon on her left shoulder; mine is on my right and curved like a capital C, like a folded ink-print of hers. But, supper over, as we tumble into our beds, where we always used to lie facing each other, now we turn away.

Badger slept on the floor between our beds, eventually settling with a huff as we ignored each other. He's an old boy, is Badger, dappled with grey and with a pronounced arthritic limp but as sharp as a tack and an expert at conning folk out of a bit of sausage or a nibble of shortbread. In the morning, at first light, he jumps on *my* bed and carefully creeps up the ruffled coverlet as if through a snowdrift, until we're nose to nose. I bury my face in his scratchy fur and squish my fingers through his soft, fluffy undercoat. I stay like this for ages, hands round his warm, solid middle, not wanting the day to begin.

I look over to Lemon's bed. Empty. Dog bobbling at my heels, I head downstairs to find her, pulling on my gloves as I go. You can't be too careful.

The kitchen table is laid for breakfast. I touch an elbow to the teapot – it's warm under its quilted cosy. The mams and Lemon must be about somewhere. My belly growls like a sad bear in a cave. Is it guilt about our fight or hunger? I don't know why I'm so out of sorts this morning . . .

Except, I completely do. It was a nasty, unkind argument and I said some awful, horrible things which I didn't mean at all. Lemon has plenty of whisperling ability, it's just hers will develop at a normal rate. Mine landed on me all at once because of the accident. And I know I couldn't do any of it without her.

I lift my glasses to rub at my eyes, wincing as a rough bit of leather on my glove scratches my eyelid, and hear Mam in my head quoting her favourite poet, Edgar Allan Poe: 'That years of love have been forgot / In the hatred of a minute'.

They always get to me, those words. Claggy pressure fills me from the chest up and I swallow hard. It's no good. Big, ploppy tears roll down my face and I scrub at my cheeks with the sleeve of my nightdress. Yuck. I need a hanky, but going back upstairs feels like really hard work.

My eyes land on Mam's 'best' bag, hung on a drawer knob on the dresser. There'll be a hanky in there. I hesitate; I shouldn't be looking in her bag without permission, but she isn't here, is she, and I'm not doing anything wrong, am I? And this is *completely* different to Lemon snooping for letters.

A moment later, Mam's bag is swaying over the crook of my arm and I'm playing at being fancy, like a fine lady in one of them London stores with the flags and the pillars outside, and the counters dripping with pearls and diamonds. I settle my finger and thumb on the gilt snap fastener and twist it. It opens pleasingly and I spend a moment snapping the bag open and closed, swinging it by its pretty chain, before remembering what I wanted it for.

I fish around for a handkerchief, and when my fingers land on soft material I pull it out. Snagged in the lace around the edge is a newspaper clipping. It's another 'missing girl' article, dated a few days after the piece Lemon showed me about Maeve. I unfold it, heart beating.

The article gives details of a girl called Florence, and another with the surname Ravenscroft, although *they* have a boy's name, which must be some sort of mistake. The piece links both cases with that of the other missing girls, mentioning possible sightings in Gloucester. And this time, there are photographs.

Breath catches in my throat. Sassy, brave girls look back at me. I can see their whisperling shine – a smudge of light just behind the temple, captured forever in silver salts and carbon. Within our family, this is something unique to me, the ability to see the mark of a whisperling in a photograph. I pull a glove off my hand with my teeth and trace their faces with my bare finger, not sure what I'm expecting to feel, but still, there's a fizz of something.

The missing girls *are* whisperlings. Lemon was right.

'Lemon!' My voice is wobbly. I replace Mam's bag, and with fumbling, jittery fingers I lift the latch and pull open the door to the main room of the pub. 'LemonLemonLemonLemonLemon!' I yell, but the pub is empty and I hop from one foot to the other, bubbling with excitement about my discovery. Where *is* everyone?

The front door opens, making me jump.

'Mornin', love. What're you looking so chipper about?' says Mam, rubbing her hands together as she enters. She's white with cold, although there's no frost on the windows this morning. She's followed by Bessie, who carries a bucket filled with red-stained rags. I look away – lady time is private and I don't want to embarrass her, but there's something odd about it . . .

'Why've you gone that way to the privy?'

'What?' Bessie looks at me and follows my gaze to the bucket. 'Oh no, this isn't –'

Mam cuts her off. 'The back door was stuck, so we had to come round the front way.'

'Um . . . yes, that's it,' agrees Bessie, hurriedly. 'Anyway, I'll get these soaking and get breakfast on. Porridge, everyone?' It's a joke – we always have porridge on a weekday – and Bessie smiles so hard it must be hurting her face.

There may be no frost, but the early-morning air is fresh enough and I rub at my arms to warm them. *Hurry up, Lem, I've got stuff to tell you!* And maybe *she* can tell me why the mams are acting so peculiarly.

'I know,' says Bessie. 'Chilly one, isn't it?' She pulls the door closed behind her. 'And grab me some milk from the cold-house, would you?'

I nod, wordlessly.

'Oh, and give your sister a shout, there's a love. She'd stay in bed all bloomin' day given half a chance. Sleeps like the dead, that one.'

## 11

No stone unturned.

That's what they say, isn't it, when looking for someone who is missing? As if you're going to go out and lift up rocks and find a whole person hiding underneath.

As soon I say 'But her bed is empty', everything changes. I wish I'd kept those words inside me a little while longer. I wish I'd had breakfast with the mams, eaten Bessie's terrible, lumpen porridge, joked again about how you could use it to fill the gaps in the window frame. Then after breakfast, I wish I'd joined Mam on her walk to the grocer's or butcher's, telling each other how this was nice, we should do this more often, we don't get to talk any more.

But I didn't. Instead I tell them Lemon's bed is empty.

'What do you mean?' Mam says.

But she knows what I mean. She is missing. Lemon is missing.

For the first few minutes we shout up the stairs, in the stables, on the towpath looking left and right, expecting to see her, anticipating the rush of relief, the annoyance, the laughter, when enough time has passed and it's stopped being a nightmare and turned into an anecdote. *Remember when Lemon took off? Oh, she's a one! Had us proper going that time.*

Minutes turn to hours and the unsettling flutter in my chest grows heavy wings. 'She'll not have gone far,' the mams say, reassuring themselves, but not me. They check the village, thinking perhaps, at first light, for reasons best known to herself, Lemon needed to go for bread or a newspaper, wilfully disobeying the mams' rule of 'Nowhere without us, not for a while.'

But no one has seen her.

At dusk, Mam grips Bessie's hand, white-knuckled and arm shaking, when Mr Black, the postmaster, offers to arrange a search party.

'Did she say anything to you, Nin? Anything at all?' I shake my head, last night's horrid argument replaying in my head so loudly I think that if Mam put her ear to mine she would hear every last spiteful word of it. I can't look at Gran, wispy and sad, shaking her head at me from her spot at the bar. The mams haven't opened the pub and the police are here, summoned by Mr Black, the kind, grey-haired postmaster who wears armless, wire-rimmed glasses that balance on the tip of his nose. Every mean, silly comment I've ever made about him adds to the loop in my brain and I feel awful, the tears prickling the back of my eyes at his decency and concern.

'We call him Penny,' I say with a sob. 'Like the stamp.'

Detective Simons stares at me and sighs. 'I'm not sure stamps are relevant,' he observes. He is a short, bored-looking man with a head as shiny as a conker and a thick, grey moustache that thins into tails that reach his ears, like two dormice. He shifts uncomfortably in his chair as Mam passes me a handkerchief and guides me away, seating me close to the bar.

As Mam settles me, Gran lays a hand on her arm, clouding Mam's bangles like mist over a valley. Mam squeezes her eyes shut and gives a little nod of recognition. When she gets back to the detective, he's still looking uninterested, but seems keen for 'refreshment', so Bessie brings him a beer.

'You had a break-in a while back, I hear,' he says, gawping at Bessie's wide-legged trousers and blood-red waistcoat. He has already asked where the man of the house is, as we knew he would. It's Mam's name above the door.

'Just kids, letting off steam,' Bessie says.

'Anything taken? Anything of value?' he asks and Bessie shakes her head. The detective nods, slowly, and writes something in his notepad.

'I've heard your girl was one of them,' he says, holding his glass to the light, examining its quality.

Mam bristles. 'One of what?' She smooths her skirts and follows the officer's eyes with her own as he looks around the pub, taking in the lumpy walls and blackened timber dotted with twinkling brasses.

'One of *them*,' he repeats. 'A creeper.'

'Does that make any difference?' asks Bessie. 'She's still missing.'

The detective pulls a face and drains his beer, wiping his mouth with the back of his hand. 'Good head on that,' he says approvingly. He puts the glass down, replaces the cap on his pen and closes his notepad. He stands up to leave.

'That's it?' Mam asks.

Simons shrugs. 'What more can we do? She'll be off having an adventure. Nothing to worry about, ladies, I'm sure. Girls like that can look after themselves.'

'*Girls like* . . .' Mam's temper strains like a greyhound out of a trap. Bessie puts a hand on her arm. I understand now why they didn't tell the police about the stolen book.

'Like, you know . . . unconventional types,' he says with a bit of a sneer, waving an arm at the mams, 'such as your good selves.' He heads for the door. 'You'll see. She'll turn up when she's hungry, or bored. They always do.'

'And what are we supposed to do in the meantime? Do you not want a photograph?'

He taps the side of his forehead. 'It's all up here,' he says. 'I'll just keep an eye out for someone that looks like that one there.' He nods at me and laughs, closing the door behind him.

We stand in shocked silence. Mam grips Bessie's hand, her knuckles white.

'Did you spit in his beer, Bessie?'

'That I did, Rose, that I did.'

Days pass and there's still no sign. I tell the mams of Lemon's interest in the missing girls – things have gone too far to keep secrets – and so they spend their days in Gloucester, combing the streets and showing Lemon's photograph in shops and cafes.

I won't tell them about the row.

I can't.

It's my fault. It's all my fault.

After a week or so, distracted by looking for Lemon, the mams loosen their grip on me. Mam in particular is wan and weary and often takes to her bed, but in spite of this they return to the city to search for her, this time staying overnight. For the first time in forever I find myself entirely alone, save

Gran, and Badger, who follows me around forlornly. The pub feels like an oversized coat and, out of place, Badger and I take a walk to the woods that shroud the pub from the rest of the village. Winter has stripped the trees of green but still the forest is dense and dark, the leafless trunks and branches crowding together like a giant game of pick-up sticks.

I know what I'm looking for and after a while I find it, a tree, knotty and swollen as if pregnant, easy to climb and comfortable to perch on. I spot our initials carved low in the bark. We were much smaller then. I kneel down in the scrubby bracken and remove a glove, running my fingers over the L and N. *Where are you, Lemon?*

I press a hand against the scratchy trunk and, in a flash, I'm back there: leaning against this very tree, eyes carefully shielded for fear of being accused of cheating, counting to fifty. *Coming, ready or not!* Crunching through the undergrowth like a snuffling boar piglet, hunting high and low for my hidden sister. But try as I might, I couldn't find her. And so, because I desperately wanted to win, and because, too, a part of me was frightened I may have lost her forever and I was all alone, I focused, *really* focused, tongue-tip jammed in the corner of my mouth, forehead pressed against the trunk in concentration as I repeated our secret saying: 'Ogethertay oreverfay, oreverfay ogethertay. Ogethertay oreverfay, oreverfay ogethertay.' Pig Latin, it's called, a daft code to confuddle grown-ups. You take the beginning of a word and swap it to the end and add an 'ay'. Such a dippy little rhyme but it worked – I *saw* the route to her; it was like a glowing ribbon threading us together, weaving through the trees, guiding me. When I found her, crouching behind a dry-stone wall at the edge of the copse, she said she had felt it too, like she was a fish on a line. It was magical. And then of course we argued because she'd gone out of the boundary and was technically cheating, but in that moment we understood. Together forever, forever together.

Would it work again, now?

I lean against the tree, forehead and hands pressed to the bark. Closing my eyes, I picture her in my mind, focus on her face, capture the feel of her in my heart. 'Ogethertay oreverfay, oreverfay ogethertay. Ogethertay oreverfay, oreverfay together–

'*Oof!*' I stumble back. *Lemon?* Her shine is so strong that it dazzles me. I blink, confused, and

66

grab for her, hand pulling through her hair, which comes away like my fingers are made of razors. Shapes scud in front of my mind's eye like racing clouds – a tiny, white building . . . that same pointy witch's hat from the last messaging – and then Lemon's face, with an expression I can't read. She shakes her head and there is an explosion of light and – *boof!* Gone. Like a door slammed in my face.

Confused and shaken, I open my eyes and straighten up, brushing leaves from my clothes. 'Come on, Badger, let's go,' I mutter.

We make our way out of the wood, twigs snapping and crunching underfoot. Suddenly, Badger growls, as a movement in the gloom makes my heart jump. The little terrier hurtles into the trees, barking manically, as a muntjac deer, squat and ears flattened, skitters from her hiding place and disappears into the woodland.

'Badger!' I yell, chasing after him, one hand on my head to keep my hat on. I pierce the dark centre of the copse and with a thumping heart realize I'm almost out at the other side, as far away from the village and the pub as it gets, at the edge of the farmland beyond.

*Stupid dog*. I just have to wait. He'll come back, trotting lopsidedly, proud of himself, soon enough. Discarded stones long tumbled from ancient, broken walls, inched out by moss and lichen, provide a makeshift seat. A circle of rocks surround what may have been a fire. I pull back my gaze. A tin can tucked under a tree stump. An area brushed clean of rubble and spiky bracken. I push at one of the large rocks with my foot.

*No stone unturned.*

Breath catches in my throat.

My sister's scarf nestles in the dirt, yellow silk smeared with a red-black stain.

Heart thumping, I tuck the scarf in my pinafore pocket. That dark crimson stain on the material. The colour of bl–

My breath catches as the crack of a twig startles me.

A shape steps into the glade. 'Were you followed?'

He brandishes a branch like a bayonet. A raggedy young man wearing trousers too short and a jacket too large, head shrouded with a shawl so his features are in shadow. But I recognize him immediately as the boy from the other week at the pub, the one who became angry when he didn't get his message.

'Were you followed?' he repeats.

I shake my head. He points to the disturbed rock. 'You can have it back. Done the job.' His fingers are filthy, ingrained with dirt.

'*Done the job?*' Blood pumps in my ears. I gulp. 'What have you done with her? Have you . . . have you finished 'er off?'

'What? No, course not. Thought about it . . . There's some what would say it'd be a kindness. She kept wigglin' an' making these awful noises an' it proper upset me. But I couldn't.'

'You animal!' I shout, voice cracking. My sister, my lovely, bright, funny sister, kidnapped by this evil boy! I stride around his camp, now I realize that's what this is, kicking over stones and pushing back bracken. 'Where is she? Where are you keeping her?' Fury propels me and I rush up to him and shove him, as hard as I can.

He stumbles backwards. 'Hey, watch it! She's fine. What the heck are you doing?'

'If she's "fine", then where is she?'

He looks at me as though I'm deranged. 'You saw her, didn't you? Runnin' away?'

I open and close my mouth like a landed fish.

'Her leg healed up nicely after I got her out of the trap. Don't need no dressing on it no more.' He arranges his gathered firewood, sits on his haunches and brings a small, brass box out of his pocket. 'So, yeah, you can have the scarf back. Not sure that blood'll come out, though.' There's lettering on the little box. THE ALLIES TINDERBOX, it says. He flicks it open, takes a pinch of material and lays it carefully on a small pile of firewood and moss and strikes the flint until it sparks. He blows gently on the embers and when it crackles to life he smiles like a child being shown a magic trick.

My head spins. 'You're talking about the muntjac.'

'Of course I'm talking about the muntjac. What d'you think I was talking about?' He lays some kindling over the smouldering moss. 'Gently does it.' His brow furrows in concentration and the pink tip of his tongue sits in the corner of his mouth. My eyes narrow. He's even younger than I'd thought, no more than a couple of years older than me. There's no way he's a soldier. I bet he stole that box from one of the Glosters when he nicked the regimental badge.

'You bin a while.'

'What do you mean?' I say.

'You said you'd come back *soon*. Bring me some more food. They were looking for me, did you know? There was a search party, so I took me boat back up to Gloucester, to me sister's, but I couldn't stay there. Too loud.' He shakes his head as if to rid himself of a noise. 'Hello, mate!'

Badger, out of breath and pleased with himself, trots up to greet him, entirely ignoring me. He sniffs the boy's ankles and allows him to scratch behind his ears until he makes a noise somewhere between a snore and a purr. I watch them, bewildered. The things I thought I knew have been thrown in the air, shot at and are coming down like shrapnel. My brain is still scrabbling to collect them together when there's a shout of 'Nin!' and the crunch of feet on bracken.

'Nin?' he says, turning to me wildly. Understanding drops into his eyes like a penny-in-the-slot machine. 'Please. I dunno what you think I've done, but please, please, get out of here!'

I hesitate. What if he *has* done something to Lemon? I spool through our exchange. 'You thought I was her,' I say, working it out. 'So you can't have killed her.'

He looks shocked. 'You thought I –' He shakes his head, stricken. 'I wouldn't do that.' The shouts get louder. 'Please, Nin, don't let them find me,' he pleads.

I nod, deciding. 'Come on, Badge,' I say, but the dog doesn't move, hypnotized after his ear-tickles. 'Come *on*!' I grab his collar and drag him away, shoving Lemon's scarf in my pocket, and when we're a safe distance from the boy's camp I shout, 'I'm over here!'

I tell the searchers that Badger had run off and I was just looking for him, and brace myself for the telling-off I'll get from the mams, who, on their return from searching for one daughter, would have found the other one gone too. I don't tell anyone about my encounter with the boy, but when I'm home I find I've dropped Lemon's scarf somewhere, and can't stop my tears from falling.

14

A few days later, Detective Simons is back.

'We suspect foul play,' he announces, delivering the news with something close to delight and rubbing the skinny mouse-tail of his moustache between two fingers like a movie villain. He takes something from his pocket: Lemon's bloodied scarf. The ground comes up to meet me and I have to sit down. What should I do? Simons waves it as if he's waving a chequered flag to start a motor car race and Mam gasps, reaching to grab it. He whips it away like he's teasing a cat.

'No, no, no,' he says, tapping his nose. 'This is *evidence*, madam. Can't have untrained civilians handling it, can we?' He scrunches it in his hands and bundles it back in his pocket. 'But you recognize the item, do you?'

Mam nods, wipes a bead of sweat from her forehead. 'It's my daughter's scarf,' she says in a whisper.

'Excellent.' Detective Simons turns the corners of his moustache between finger and thumb. 'As I had deduced, eh, Hagley?'

Wearily, Woman Police Constable Hagley, one of a small number of female police officers in the county, half smiled then turned to my mother. 'I'm very sorry, Mrs Esmond. We'll do everything we can to –'

'We'll catch the scoundrel who did this, you can be sure of it, dear lady. We'll likely pin the other murders on him as well. Send him for the long drop.'

'*Other* murders?' asks Bessie.

Detective Simons waves a hand, dismissively. He wears a signet ring on his pinkie, engraved with swirly initials. An R and a T, maybe. 'Those other missing girls. Probably dead.'

WPC Hagley drops her pencil. 'Sir! We don't know that –'

'Oh, come now. Penny to a pound it was the same fellow. They get a taste for it, don't they? Like Jack the Ripper.'

Blood thuds in my ears. There will be another search of the woods and this time they won't stop until they find something. What should I do? If I tell the mams of my encounter with this boy, they'll want to find him, and that will scare him off. And if I tell this idiot detective . . . well, he's already made his mind up. Typical rozzer. That's probably what the initials on his ring stand for.

I think of my sister. *What would Lemon do?* Both of the newspaper articles – the one Lemon showed me, and the one I found in Mam's handbag that's now tucked under my pillow – mention possible sightings of the missing girls in Gloucester. I know the mams have already searched there, but I just have a feeling . . . And then there was that flash of something when I tried to connect to Lemon, that witch's hat. There is something very familiar about it I can't quite put my finger on.

What would Lemon do? The answer is obvious. I have to go to Gloucester. If Lemon is anywhere, she's there.

The following morning I'm up long before the first birdsong. In fact, it's so dark the only bird-noise I hear is the *twit-twoo* of an owl. With shaking fingers, I light an oil lamp and by its milky glow pack a small knapsack with a fresh set of underwear, a clean petticoat, knee socks and an extra cardigan. I drag the suitcase of dressing-up clothes out from under Lemon's bed and flip it open, allowing myself the briefest of smiles. Lemon usually bundles her clothes into balls and shoves them into our chest of drawers. But not these. These items are neatly folded and separated with tissue paper and, un-gloved, I work my way through them, layer by layer, each touch causing a scene from a previous owner's life to flash into my head: a beautiful girl in a monocle; a strange, captivating house; the creak of rope . . . Where *did* these clothes come from?

I find what I'm looking for – a waxed navy-blue cotton cape with a hood – and bundle it under my arm. I ruffle Badger's fur; I'd thought briefly he'd come with me, but I can't take him from the mams, and besides, he's an old boy now and it wouldn't be fair to drag him to the city. Holding the lamp in front of me, I creep down to the kitchen. I pack an apple, a hunk of bread and a slice of ginger cake for myself, and some more bread, potted meat and a can of potatoes as leverage for the first part of my plan. That should be plenty. I'll only be gone a day or so. I'll find Lemon and bring her home.

'What on earth are you doing?'

Bessie, in yesterday's clothes, places on the kitchen table a tray laden with sweet-smelling tinctures, scrunched-up cloths, cups, bowls and a brown glass bottle labelled QUININE. With a pair of wooden tongs, she wordlessly plops the rags into the laundry bin, pours hot water from the kettle into the sink and washes her hands with carbolic soap. I hadn't even noticed the kettle was on.

I'd heard Mam coughing overnight; she's hasn't been right since her early return from Gloucester. 'I hoped she'd shaken it off but last night she went downhill. Maybe talking to the police took it out of her,' explains Bessie, wearily, drying her hands and sitting down at the table. 'She's fighting it, but . . .'

I ignore the way Bessie says 'but', with eyes glassy and red-rimmed. The word hangs there like a grenade with a loose pin.

And what if *it* is the Spanish flu? Bessie doesn't say, and I don't ask. The mams say not to call it that at all given it only got its name because newspapers

78

in Spain were able to openly report on it, everywhere else too fearful of lowering morale with yet more bad news.

'Lemon's in Gloucester,' I tell her, fiddling with the buckle on my knapsack. 'I know it.'

I expect her to tell me to leave it to them.

I expect her to tell me not to go.

We hear Mam cough upstairs in her room, dry and rattly. Bessie's shoulders drop, and she nods, as if answering a question she has silently asked herself. 'I can't leave her,' she says. 'Not until the fever breaks. Otherwise I'd come with you.'

It takes a beat before I realize she's giving me permission to go. Alone.

'You've got two days,' she says, standing up to walk over to open a drawer, from which she takes out a purse. 'Then I want you back here. Take the bus; there's one from the village first thing. Ask at the post office. Make sure you stay somewhere decent, a proper B and B.' She presses some coins into my palm.

'What about Mam?' My voice catches. 'What will she say?'

'You leave your mam to me. I'll tell her when she's rested some more.'

'Oh, Bessie . . . she's not –' *Dying*. I want to say 'dying'. But I can't. Because what if Bessie says yes?

'Now, don't you go worrying. She'll be better when both of her girls are home safe.'

I know not to ask again.

'And remember, two days and not a minute more, mind, or I'll have your guts for garters.' Bessie smiles and squeezes my hand. 'If anyone can find her,' she says, 'you can, Nin.' I nod in reply, unable to speak, scared that the fear that jumped from Bessie's hands to mine will never leave me. Bessie turns and climbs back up the stairs to see to Mam.

Moments later I yank on my gloves and pull the cape over my shoulders, fastening it on the inside. It was too big for Lemon the last time she tried it on. I catch sight of myself reflected in the window. It fits me perfectly.

It's still dark when I leave The Bargeman's. There's no direct path through the copse to the boy's camp, and any moonlight is clogged by dense, rumbling cloud. The bus would be easier and I'm loath to disobey Bessie – if she realizes I've already left she'll have a fit – but my agitated legs need to move and there's a chance that if I linger I might chicken out. Besides, this boy knows something, I'm sure of it. I've rehearsed my speech; the boy is to take me to Gloucester in his boat in return for my silence on his whereabouts. It's a fair offer, given that he would already have been discovered if Detective Simons weren't so slow-witted, but it won't be long before the policeman arranges a search of the woods. 'Our Detective Simons couldn't find his backside without a map,' commented Bessie after his earlier visit.

Am I right to believe this boy, when he says he hasn't hurt my sister? He seemed genuine enough, but what if he believes he hasn't hurt her, but actually he has, in a moment of madness or by way of accident? The way he's living isn't normal, and his skittishness . . . it troubles me. He may not have anything to do with Lemon's disappearance, but I can't escape the nagging feeling that he's done *something*.

I pick my way through the trees, ears pricking at every sound. It's no noisier than in the daytime, but the blanket of night shuts your eyes and opens your ears, and innocent snuffles and crunches become chilling snarls and heart-stopping crashes. I sniff. A baby-dragon puff of campfire wafts under my nose. I'm going the right way.

Eventually, the trees thin, the sight of fields opening out beyond is like an exhale, and –

'Don't move!' I'm grabbed round the neck and yanked off my feet, the point of something pressing into my throat.

'Don't hurt me!' I rasp, fingers digging against the arm to try and prise it from my windpipe. 'I've told the mams where I am . . . If I'm not back soon, they'll be up here with the rozzers!'

He pushes me off and I land with a thud on the ground. 'You stupid idiot, I could have —'

'What?' I inhale deeply, pulling in as much air as I can. 'Killed me?' I rub at my throat. 'That really hurt.'

He throws the 'knife' — a stubby twig — to the ground and kicks it into the trees. 'Yeah, well, it serves you right. Creepin' up on folk like that s'askin' fer trouble.'

I can't say I don't feel a bit silly. I get to my feet. 'Here,' I say. 'Brought you some food.' I hold out the paper bag, which he snatches wordlessly, a brief smile passing over his face when he opens it. He rips off a chunk of bread. 'You're welcome,' I say, sarcastically.

'Fanks.' He holds the bread up like he's saying *Cheers!* and immediately I feel silly again, demanding a show of good manners from someone so desperate. 'What d'you want, then?' he adds.

'How do you know I want something?' I choose the biggest, flattest rock, brush it off with my gloved hand and sit down.

He raises an eyebrow and sits opposite me. 'I've met your type before.'

*

'No way. I'm to take you nowhere.' He doesn't look at me, instead riddles the dregs of his fire with a stick. 'I mean, thanks fer the bread an' all, but no. Why the 'eck would I?'

I take a breath and clench my shoulders. 'Because if you don't, I'll tell the police about you and you'll be arrested for kidnap, and I can't say they wouldn't be keen to pin a few more murders on you an' all.'

He shrinks back and drops the stick into the fire with shaking hands. 'I ain't murdered nobody. Why d'you keep saying that?'

'Well, I've half a mind to believe you, but look at it my way. *Something's* happened to my sister and you're mixed up in it. Somehow. Maybe you are completely innocent, or maybe –' I narrow my eyes – '*maybe* you're being clever, in the way of a wicked murderer, and trying to throw me off the scent!'

'No! I wouldn't do tha'! I'm not killin' no one, you can't make me!'

'What?'

The boy's eyes are wild and it's like we're having two entirely different conversations. 'But I'm not going to *make* you kill anybody . . . What are you on about? Hey! Wait, where are you going? Come back!'

He's already on his feet. He kicks dirt over the remains of the fire, grabs a small knapsack and the food I gave him, and sprints off through the trees.

I finally catch up with him at the ships' graveyard. It's an eerie collection of purposely scuttled boats about a mile upstream of the woods, where the hulks have been rammed up the bank to reinforce the divide between the controlled, efficient canal and the River Severn, its wildly ill-mannered neighbour.

The boy isn't far ahead, but I have to cross the canal via a footbridge to get to him and my legs won't move at all. Stupid, stupid water! Stupid, stupid me. I picture Lemon's face in my mind, urging me to *Come on, Nin!* I scrunch my eyes and tap a toe on the bridge, as if testing a hot bath. The water is visible through the metal lattice under my feet so I squeeze my eyes fully shut. It's the only way. I carefully lift and lower one foot after the other like a show pony, making sure I don't trip over anything, and as soon as I get to the other side I scrabble up the verge to relieve myself behind a patch of ferns.

If he saw my performance, he doesn't mention it. He stands on the deck of a snubby tug, similar in shape but half the size of a narrowboat and engine-powered, made for dragging several boats and their cargo at once. He plucks a long piece of grass from the verge and shoves it between his teeth, rolling it from side to side like a cow.

'I'm sorry,' I say when I finally get to him. 'What I meant was, when we find 'er you'll be off the hook, and everyone will know you haven't killed anyone.'

'Lucky old me.'

He untethers the mooring line, winding it expertly round his elbow and hand and placing it over a hook on the deck. It would have been a pretty little boat once. Painted roses and castles are just about visible under a layer of grime. The boat's name at least, threaded prettily through a spray of bright pink blossom, looks like it's regularly wiped clean. *Melody*. Hand-painted crotchets and quavers dance around the M and Y.

'Named after me mam,' he explains. He holds a hand out for me to climb aboard and I take it. 'And I'm Wilf. Wilf Trindle.' He glances at my black gloves. I'm grateful to be wearing them; even through the leather I can feel a wash of fear and sadness from him. This boy may not be a ghost, but he's haunted, nonetheless.

I don't really remember Wilf, but I do remember his boat. I close my eyes. Memories of it are at half-height, and I mainly recall all the things that twinkled, just like a child would do. It was lovely, his boat, like a fairy's grotto, speckled with shiny trinkets in copper and brass. Brightly painted plates hung from the walls and delicate crochet mats were scattered on surfaces like snowflakes. Outside, watering cans decorated with flowers edged the deck, like a garden made of tin.

Wilf pulls a rag from his pocket, opens the wheelhouse door and disappears. I follow him. It's a tiny space inside, but neat and clean, unlike the rest of the boat, which seems to have melted in on itself.

'After Ma died, Pa used all the space fer cargo, save a bunk to sleep in,' Wilf explains. A pile of blankets is folded up in one corner.

Wilf is crouching in the engine space, his nose level with my ankles. He rubs at an already gleaming brass valve and tucks the rag back into his breast pocket, where it flops near his lapel as if he were a gentleman.

'Why do you bother with the woods? Why don't you just sleep on here?' I ask him.

'I do, sometimes, but it's freezin' on 'ere, ain't you noticed?' He blows out a breath as if pretending to smoke. 'Can't have a proper fire. An' s'all right fer squirts like you an' your sister, but I don't fit that well.' It's true, the wheelhouse is the size of our kitchen table, just about long enough to lie out in. 'I'll do 'er up proper one day,' he says, 'when Pa gets back.'

'Is he –' I don't want to ask. 'Still at war?'

'Missin', so they say.' He clamps his mouth shut and I take the hint and stop asking.

The tugboat starts with ease, the thrum of the engine vibrating noisily. Wilf shuts the hatch and it deadens it a bit but it's still hard to talk above the noise.

'What made you change your mind? About taking me to Gloucester, I mean.'

'You're right: if we find 'er, then I'm off the hook. An' until then it might be a good idea fer me to keep movin' fer a bit. I'll go up to Birmingham, maybe further, lie low until it's blown over. And she's all right, your sister – Clemency, Lemon, whatever you call her. Reminds me of my niece, she does. She helped me. Brought me some food.'

A small piece of the puzzle slots into place. ''Er early-morning walks – she was meeting up with you,' I say. And then another, more horrifying, thought enters my head. '*Urgh*, you two . . . you're not –' I can barely think it, let alone say it – '*sweethearts*, are you?'

'*Flamin' Nora!* Course not –' There's a clatter and thump as the boat swerves to the left, then rights itself as Wilf gains control. 'No! I just said she reminds me *of my niece*.' He shakes his head briskly, as if throwing off the terrible suggestion. 'Tha's proper off, tha'.'

'Sorry,' I say, just as embarrassed.

'Scared 'er half to death, though, the first time she stumbled over me in them woods.' He grins. 'Though it'd kill 'er to admit it.' He pauses, points at something. 'There's your pub.'

As we chug past, moonlight collides with early-morning sun to create a strange effect on the whitewashed wall. On the usually plain white side wall, there's an odd pink smudge, almost like a blurry letter C. *A trick of the light as night turns to day*, I think. Homesickness pulls at my heart, which, given I've only been gone a short while, is possibly a bit daft.

'Did you really tell 'em where you were goin'?'

I nod. I won't tell him Bessie thinks I'm getting to Gloucester on the bus in about an hour or so. Not saying much is easier at the moment than the truth – that perhaps Bessie let me leave to find Lemon because Mam is sicker than she's letting on – but it irritates Wilf, who shakes his head. 'Oh well, tha's all right then. They'll definitely not be out of their minds frettin' tha' they've lost *another* daughter.' He glares at me, like an annoyed older brother. 'Honestly, you an' your sister are a pair of idiots – an' I'm a bigger idiot for goin' along with you.' He wags a finger at me, his knitted fingerless gloves fraying at the edges.

I fold my arms, irritated in my turn by the insult, until a sudden lurch reminds me of the water underneath my bottom. I swallow a mouthful of sick.

'For goodness' sake, sit somewhere you can see the horizon, it'll stop you wantin' to gip.'

I haul myself up on to a bench built into the side of the cabin. After a few minutes' staring forward ('towards the bow') my stomach settles.

'Better?' asks Wilf.

I nod grudgingly.

'You're doing better'n I thought you would.'

'What do you mean?'

'For one so scared of the water. Why don't you like it?'

'How do you know I don't?'

'You're kidding, right?' Wilf snorts. 'You practically glued yourself to the verge on the way to the boat, an' I've never seen anyone cross a bridge like that.'

A scorch of embarrassment burns up my neck and flames my cheeks. It matters less that Wilf saw me prancing ridiculously. What if he heard me *wee*? I hate the water, but right now I'm considering jumping off the boat and swimming back home.

'I fell in, a while ago,' I say, telling him the brief version of events. 'It somehow made me more . . . *available* to ghosts and –' I shake away the memory of the water in my lungs, and how it burned. 'And yes, it's made me hate the canal. I wish we could move,' I say aloud for the first time.

Wilf thoughtfully chews his grass, one hand on the rudder and the other turning a catch to slide down the cabin window. He spits a green gob into the water and pushes the window back up, 'I understand tha',' he says quietly. 'What about them?'

He means my gloves. I turn my hands to look at them. 'Protection,' I say, hoping that'll be enough, but I feel Wilf's eyes on me, expectantly. 'Sometimes I can feel more, through my hands, like memories and things.' I shrug. 'More of the ghost stuff gets through when I'm not wearing them.' I laugh, flatly. 'Like I haven't got enough of that to deal with! It's weird. I don't really understand it.'

He falls quiet for a moment. 'If I gave you something of me mam's, you'd be able to . . . to feel her?'

'Maybe,' I say. 'If you wanted me to try, I –'

'No, no. Thanks, but no. She said everything she wanted to say when she were alive. Proper chatterbox she were.' He smiles, but sadness rolls from him. He nudges me in the belly. 'It'd be no good to me, you being the one to see her. It's me tha' misses her, ain't it?'

I nod, trying not to cry. I push my own mother's face out of my mind. She'll be *fine*, Bessie promised.

'So, how long have you been doing the boat up for?' I ask, changing the subject.

'Three or four months. Since I bin back.' He breaks into a smile. 'She goes well an' all. Had 'er up to three knots I 'ave.'

I nod, impressed. 'Back from where, exactly?'

He looks at me as if my head is on backwards. 'From France! From the front.'

I laugh, in that strange, nervous way that sometimes happens when you're told terrible news. 'No,' I say. He *can't* have been in France. 'You're –' I wave a hand up and down, like he's a fence I'm painting. I can't find the words. 'How old are you?' He's tall, yes, but he's obviously not eighteen, so it isn't possible that he's been at war. There's barely a shadow on his chin and no whisker to be seen.

'Fourteen.'

The information is like a slap. 'Four*teen*?' Two years older than me. 'But . . . you're still a *child*,' I say. 'How could you have been fighting in France?'

'I weren't the only one. They were a lot less fussy about the rules by the time I signed up,' he says bluntly. 'By the time I went over, they were 'aving to practically drag men off the streets to go an' fight, what with everyone knowin' what it was really like out there by then. Couldn't get me signed up fast enough, they couldn't.' Wilf scuffs at the floor with his foot. 'They wanted boatmen and I was a good 'un.'

I knew that much was true. Boatmen were The Bargeman's best customers and the mams said we'd 'lost a yup of 'em' so that the canal routes in France could run smoothly.

'How long?'

'Eighteen months, give or take.' He scuffs again at an invisible mark on the floor with his boot. 'Went to look for me dad, didn't I.'

'Did you find any sign of him?' I ask, gently.

He shakes his head. So that must be why he came to the pub that night, to the messaging. Lemon must have told him we could help get a message from his father, should the worst have happened to him.

I can't speak, my voice crushed by all of the things I'm feeling. I'm feeling stupid for doubting him, guilty for thinking he'd stolen his regimental badge, and blazingly angry that this boy had to go through all that at all. I know now why it was so difficult to look him in the eye. Though his body has barely seen fourteen years, his eyes hold the pain of a thousand lifetimes.

A whisper of morning sun slides over the canal.

'I'm so sorry, Wilf.'

He nods in reply, and we chug on towards Gloucester in silence.

'This is as far as she can go.'

It's working boats only in the main basin of Gloucester docks, and so Wilf secures the *Melody* to the side of the canal. He's wrapped a scarf round his head, tying the ends of it over his ears. I have to shout at him to make him hear me over the engine and he flinches.

'Sorry,' I say.

I don't like the water; he doesn't like noise. What a fine pair we make.

To my left are the docks, and to my right is the twisty canal we've chugged along for *hours*. The contrast is quite something: nature ends where the docks begin. Everything here is metal and man-made, and colours slide away from greens and browns to greys and black. I run a finger round a circular rivet as large as my fist. There must be thousands of them just on this bridge alone, which is easily the length of the pub. Dark, looming warehouses block out the low winter sun and the temperature has dipped enough to make me shiver. I count at least six warehouses from here on the road bridge, and there must be a dozen more beyond that I can't see. I squint; is there anything that looks or feels familiar? But no, there's nothing.

Wilf was right to cover his ears: the noise is astonishing; there's movement *everywhere*. Shouts echo around the basin – an area about the size of a small lake where cargo is offloaded – and bounce around my ears. Dockworkers scurry over mountainous piles of sacks like mice in a barn. I rock back on my heels, nerves fluttering in my chest.

Wilf says we're to go to his sister's house first. 'She'll skin me if she knows I bin to town an' not called in,' he said with a laugh. After that, the plan is to check as many possible places for Lemon as we can, as quickly as possible, and then Wilf will make his way up the canal to Birmingham. Once I find Lemon, Bessie's money will cover a hansom cab home. We haven't discussed what I'm to do if we don't locate my sister and I'm pondering that when I hear Wilf shout.

I hurry back down the towpath. 'What is it?' I ask, drawing alongside the boat, slightly out of puff.

'Engine problems. It's nothing complicated, but I'd rather fix it now in case we need to leave smartish.'

'Can I help?' I step back aboard. It's easier this time and I feel a rush of pride.

'Chuck us a wrench, will you, please?' says Wilf. 'There's a toolbox in there, under the blankets, right-hand side.'

I open up the storage box and shift a pile of bedding to one side, snapping my hand away from something that looks animally. 'Yuck!' *Is it a rat? A –* gulp – *dead rat?* I look more closely. No, no, it's not. An icy-cold feeling trickles down my neck as I reach into the recess and take out a clump of balled-up hair. It unfurls like a black velvet ribbon.

This is my sister's hair. Even through my gloves, it pulses with her.

'What did you do?' I scream. I brandish Lemon's hair like a terrible trophy. 'You stole her ponytail!'

'Don't be a gonk. Why the 'eck would I do tha'?' He laughs, and I back away, shoving Lemon's hair into my knapsack.

'Well, I'm keeping it anyway. It's evidence!'

'Evidence of what? I haven't done anything, you banana,' he says. 'Nin, no, wait – let me explain!'

But I don't believe him, and, terrified, I jump off the boat and make for the bridge.

Oh Lemon! *What has happened to you?*

# 17

I tuck myself between two huge steel struts, hand clamped to my mouth, as if Wilf could hear my breathing over the noise of the docks. After a few moments to catch my breath, I peek out. I can't see him anywhere. Uncertainty spins round my body. *Where should I go?*

We spent a day in Gloucester not long after school shut on account of the flu, to 'soak up some local history', but afterwards Bessie said that it was mainly because trying to teach us algebra at home did her bloody head in. So I know from that trip that somewhere in the docks is a tiny, pale-coloured seafarers' chapel, famous for embracing the lively, multicultural maritime community that it sits in the middle of.

Would someone there help me? Mam said there's been problems in the past between certain members of the Church and whisperlings, but perhaps, if that chapel really does accept all comers, I could –

*Peeeeeeeeeep!*

My stomach leaps and falls like the striker at a fairground strongman game.

'Oi! You there!'

'Who, me, Officer?'

'Yeah, you,' says the red-faced policeman, whistle still between his teeth. He removes it and gives it a shake, flicking a gob of spit to the floor. In his other hand he clutches some scrunched-up paper. 'What're you up to, hanging about 'ere all by yourself?'

'I'm not –' I begin, looking around, wondering if I should tell him about Wilf and show him my sister's hair. I gesture towards a tram stop just beyond the bridge. 'I'm just off home.'

The policeman looks me up and down. 'What's with the cape? You escaped from Coney Hill or somewhere?' He means the local loony bin – the lunatic asylum – and it's a mean joke.

A prickle scratches at the back of my neck, distracting me. In the water below, the messy wash from the boats in the dock churns and foams. Breath catches in my throat – there's movement down there. I take a step back, as light spots dance behind my eyes and it's like I'm back at the pub during the last messaging, seeing those strange images. Glinting speckles appear and disappear in the rise and fall of the water. Reflections, maybe, from the windows of the surrounding buildings. I blink hard, trying to clear my vision. It looks like . . . a paper chain of cut-out dolls, I think, linked together and reaching for me from the water . . .

'You listening to me?' says the policeman. I nod, but I'm not, not really. He takes a step towards me, waving his papers at me like I'm a fly he's trying to swat. But they aren't papers, they're the posters of missing children, scrunched between his sausage-like fingers. He sees me looking.

''Ere, you ain't one of them creepers too, are yer?' My cheeks burn at the old insult. 'You *are*, ain't yer!' He makes a grab for me, and I jump out of the way.

'*Run!*' says a voice.

*Lemon?* I look round. It's not her. If it were her, she'd be here, dragging me away to safety.

'*Run!*'

It's more than one voice. It's *them*, in the water! Whatever they are, mouths opening and closing in grotesque unison –

'*RUN!*'

*Ting-ting!* The tram!

'I have to go, Mister Officer, my tram –', but he lunges for me again, as if to seize me this time. I sidestep and he clatters to the floor. I hesitate for a moment . . . should I help him up? He *is* a policeman . . . but he flails like an upturned turtle and makes a grab for my leg. I kick him, apologize, and run, the shriek of his whistle ringing in my ears as the tram pulls away without me.

I run until my lungs scorch and legs deaden, dark teeth of fear snapping at my heels. *Dead things in the water, there were dead things in the water* – pant, pant – *Dead. Things. In. The. Water!* I've never seen anything like it before: the canal boiling with spirits, like a pod of ghoulish dolphins.

It isn't just the water; there are spirits everywhere here. The streets beyond the docks teem with people and, scattered among the swarms of solid, scurrying humans, are pallid, sheeny ghosts, drifting in and out of focus, heads turning to stare at me like I've shouted out their names. I feel like a mouse ready to be plucked by a swooping ghost-gull. Or trampled by a cart or a tram or a person. The tang of horse dung and choking diesel fumes from motor cars and the huge dockside machinery makes me gag, and the acrid stench from open drains is so thick to be almost chewable. I pull the neck of my jumper up over my nose, the scent of a stolen squirt of Mam's Yardley perfume somewhat comforting.

Fear quivers my innards, but then a thought strikes me. I step into a shop doorway and slip off a glove, open my knapsack and touch my fingers to my sister's locks of hair. I close my eyes: shapes scud across my inner vision like storm clouds but when I try to focus on one it sweeps away. 'Ogethertay oreverfay, oreverfay ogethertay,' I chant, frantically. 'Ogethertay oreverfay, oreverfay ogethertay!'

It works.

In the snap of a finger I feel her. I gasp and clutch the hair to my chest. 'Lemon?' I whisper. 'Where *are* you?' I squeeze her hair and reach and reach and reach into my mind and there's a flash of that damned witch's hat and then – *oof!* – the door slams in my face again.

With a thud, I realize.

*It isn't a witch's hat . . .*

My sister is alive.

My sister is in Gloucester.

My sister does *not* want me to find her.

Shaken, I lean back against the door frame and look out at the city before me. I know what I'm looking for now and, sure enough, in a break in the clouds emerges a huge, square tower soaring skywards, its four corners each topped by a pinnacle. *The witch's hats of my visions!*

The *peeeeep!* of a policeman's whistle is the only starter signal I need.

# 18

Gloucester Cathedral with its pinnacled tower emerges from the fog and drizzle like a gothic palace and I'm so happy to see it I could almost cry. Its windows shine with what seems like the light of a thousand candles, an extravagance when times are so hard, but it's such a beautiful sight it's easy to forgive. It's like the sun has been trapped within – I reach up a hand, expecting to be warmed. It's a world away from the grime of the docks.

The sweep of dwellings on College Green edging the west side of the cathedral are like something from a Christmas card; all it needs is a sprinkling of snow. Their garden paths are swept and pristine, their front doors painted in glossy military reds and lustrous navy blues. Neatly trimmed spheres of potted bay trees stand sentry next to several doors and the privet hedges are trimmed so neatly the gardener must have used a set-square to shape the right angles so precisely. Brass plaques set under matching bell-pulls let you know that this is the home of a magistrate, this the office of a solicitor, or dentist or cleric or merchant. The yolky warmth of lamplight glows through the grey morning from gleaming windows and I breathe, feeling safe. These are the houses of good people. The perfect place to start the search for my sister.

A door opens and familiar noises and smells float out – a puff of friendly chatter, the savoury aroma of a bubbling stockpot, the smokiness of a smouldering fire. Then comes a smiling man with white hair and enormous, wing-like sideburns. The doorplate says that a doctor lives here; there's a swirly cross-like symbol to the right of his name. This must be him.

I sink with relief and open my mouth to say hello, just as a panful of lumpy, fetid water hits me in the face. I spit out a curl of potato peel. A sob spools up from my chest. It wasn't a smile he'd been offering, it was a grimace.

'Get out of here, or I'll call the law on you!' he hisses.

'I'm not doing anything wrong! I'm in town to find my sister. She looks like me. Have you seen her?'

He pauses, considering me, and for a moment I think he's going to help me.

'Hop it! If you don't get away from here this minute, the next thing I throw at you will be the pot from under my bed!' The door slams in my face.

Foul-smelling water drips from my chin and I angrily flick bits of vegetable peel from my hair and clothes. How dare he – he doesn't even know me, so why would he do that? Thankfully, my old cape is hardy and with a few shakes it's dry, but my hair is quite wet and my head and face are tight with cold. I put a hand in my pocket to check I still have the money Bessie gave me. I don't know if the cathedral was just a landmark to guide me to Gloucester or signified something more, but I won't be any use here if I die of hypothermia. I'll find a cafe, have a pot of tea and dry myself off. There's one close by in Westgate Street that I've been to with Mam that does the best lardy cake, so I head there, via an old stone archway a few steps away from College Green.

It looks like a street straight out of medieval times. The narrow cobbled lane runs pin-straight, edged with black-and-white half-timbered buildings that lean towards each other as if sharing gossip about their occupants. I pause, blood thudding in my ears. This lane is *ancient*. It's like looking into an enchanted mirror where reflections are locked in for eternity. Ghosts materialize and cluster around me, wearing outfits I've only read about in history books – elaborate Tudor ruffs, pantaloons and breeches. A beaky-masked plague doctor knocks on a door with a silver-tipped cane, and a shout from an upstairs window warns me to *Scoot!* before a chamber pot is emptied on to the cobbles below.

I stare at the ground and wrap my arms round myself, tucking my hands under my arms in case I accidentally brush against something that throws me further into the spirit world. Places like this *prove* that I'm right to wear my gloves. Imagine how overwhelmed I'd be if I took them off?

I press my back into a shop doorway, stepping away from the churning street for a moment. A sweet scent, like garden mulch and lavender, seeps through the door frame and I press my nose to it and breathe in deeply. The shop is entirely boarded up; planks of wood have been nailed over the windows and door. *What a shame*, I think, because it's a pretty little place. I look up to read the sign. KIP'S BOOKSHOP: NEW & ANTIQUE BOOKS it says, painted in swirls of navy and gold. It's the first shop past the archway and almost absorbed into the ancient gates. Its quaint and neat, red-bricked to knee height, and only about five of my strides wide. The window frames are painted black and when I press an eye to a gap in the boards I gasp in delight. Though the glass is smudged with something red, behind the smear the display is elegant and thoughtful. Piles of neatly stacked books are dotted with appropriately witty accessories. *The Tale of Pigling Bland*, *Rebecca of Sunnybrook Farm* and *The Wind in the Willows* are stacked together among knitted pigs and sheep and a charming toy car in which a felt-crafted Mr Toad sits wearing a tiny peaked hat.

'Well, Mr Kip, perhaps when you reopen I'll return,' I say, stepping away from the shop, but I immediately step back again. The difference is unmistakable. It's as if there's an invisible screen between the shop and the lane. It's pulling me in; if I lean on the door, perhaps I'll sink through it, like Gran does. I press myself against the glossy-painted wood but nothing happens. Feeling silly, I take a step back and instead try to peek again through the gap in the boards. Paint. Red paint. Someone has tried to clean it off but it's unmistakable; this beautiful window was daubed with the shape of the letter C. I suddenly remember the mark on the side of the pub as Wilf and I chugged past on the boat, for where the walls were usually gleaming white, one was pink, like a jam stain on a napkin. Is that what Mam and Bessie had been doing when I caught them with the bucket of red rags that fateful day Lemon went missing? Scrubbing the wall clean of red paint?

Did someone mark our house and this shop, like we have the plague?

I walk out of the lane and into the main street. A drop of water splats on my nose and a rumble of thunder growls like distant gunfire. I lift my hood to shield myself from the steady *plop plop* of rain and catch sight of another red paint mark, this time on the butcher's, gruesome against the backdrop of dangling, headless pheasants and fleshy slabs of pork.

'Terrible, isn't it?' says a girl's voice, well spoken but with a gentle West Country accent. She appeared as if from nowhere – small and neat, wearing a cape not dissimilar from my own but floor length and in the richest mossy green, the exact colour of the forest floor in autumn.

'Look,' she says, gesturing up and down the street. 'It's happening more and more. How awful for these poor people.' Her voice, honeyed and buttery, melts over me like I'm a crumpet; she is warmth and softness in this increasingly unwelcoming place. 'Oh my! What happened to you?' She removes a chunk of carrot from my shoulder and reaches into her pocket. 'Here,' she says, passing me a handkerchief. 'People can be so cruel, can't they?'

I nod, trying not to cry, and press at my eyes with the cotton square. 'What does it mean, the red paint?' Similar splashily painted symbols mark at least half a dozen premises on the high street. 'It looks like –' I squint – 'a letter C?'

The girl moves closer to me, the edge of her cape darkening with rainwater as it brushes the ground. 'That's exactly what it is,' she says. Her hood shadows her face, but she sounds young, maybe only three or four years older than me. 'A letter C. For "Creeper".'

Icy fingers scratch at my spine. 'Wh-what?'

'Folk are afraid of what they don't understand,' she says, lifting a hand to adjust her cloak. Her gloves are red, with tiny covered buttons and a bow at the wrist, and as she pushes back her hood for the first time I see her pale, pretty face, her slightly pointed nose, and my breath catches, for this girl has the unmistakable shine of a whisperling. And it's the brightest, most dazzling glow I have ever, ever seen.

'Wait!' I say as she walks away. A group of people spill from an alleyway on to the main street obscuring my view and I'm bumped and jostled as I strain my neck to keep sight of her. '*Oof*, watch out!' A handful of jeering, gobby schoolboys are suddenly in my way.

'Go on, biff him in the noggin!' says one, as a large man grabs a scrappy-looking boy by the collar of his ragged coat and shoves him against a wall. '"*Biff him in the noggin*"?' I tut to myself. Why can't posh people just talk proper?

The small boy pinned to the wall by the fists of the large man throws me a disarming smile and I misstep, stumbling over my feet. He is freckled, or grubby, it's hard to tell. I should help, but what can I possibly do? I put my head down and walk by.

'Mister, come on, don't hurt me!'

The boy's words tug at my conscience, and I slow my pace.

'You ain't one of 'em. Give us me money back, you thieving little rat!' The man allows the boy to drop and the lad holds his hands up in what looks like a gesture of defeat, but the smirk on his face makes me question his sincerity.

'I is! I *is*! Takes a while fer them spirits to come through. You can't expect 'em to just perform like that!'

In spite of my discomfort at the boy's treatment, and my irritation at the con he's trying to pull, I hide a smile. He's no whisperling, but it isn't a million miles away from something Lemon would say.

'Give the little rotter a thwack from us, my good man,' says one of the schoolboys, nudging his pal in the ribs. 'That sort deserves what's coming to him!' His friends bray like donkeys.

'Snobby bullies,' I mutter. They are, as Bessie would say, a 'sorry reflection on the state of the public school system', and I find myself on the side of the boy – even if he is pretending to be a whisperling.

But it isn't just his predicament that's caught my attention. The back of my neck prickles. A girl, her hair in messy, ribbon-tied bunches, and wearing a blue, unseasonably summery dress, greying socks scrunched around her ankles, joyfully twirls on the pavement. She's a pretty, freckled little thing and my heart warms to her as she dances, untroubled by the unfolding drama. It was her, I think, who drew me in.

'It's true, mister! You gotta give 'em time to gets comfortable wiv us, like.'

The angry man, large and square in body as well as head, steps towards the boy. My body tenses. Mam and Bessie say you should never punch down, but this seems to be what is about to happen. It's not going to be a fair fight. Mr Brick-head grabs the boy by his coat collar again and shoves him up against the wall with a thud.

'Hey!' The shout leaves my mouth before my brain has had the chance to realize it's a bad idea. I step back to hide, but it's too late, Mr Brick-head has seen me. His face darkens from crimson to claret, as if being boiled from the inside.

'You one of them too? You want some as well?'
He takes a step towards me, scraping the little lad
across the wall like a cleaning rag as he moves. I
could duck and run, but fear has wiped the bravado
from the boy's face. He's young, no older than seven
or eight, so I stand my ground. The man comes at
me, thunder-faced and growling, and when he's
close enough to feel his breath on my face I slip off
a glove and press it to his chest.

*Whommm!*

Blood thuds in my ears and I step outside of
myself and see his child, a girl. She looks like a little
bird, thin and paper-skinned. I feel his pain as he
kneels at her bedside, his enormous square-shaped
head resting on her pillow, watching her chest rise
and fall, rise and fall, until it stills, a howl of pain
coming from the depths of him then. I fall back,
yanking my hand away. His pain is too much; it is
alive, like an animal he keeps caged inside him.

'Eliza,' I murmur.

His fist opens and he drops the lad and the rage
falls from his face like a sheet pulled from the line.
'What did you say?'

'Eliza.' I am woozy, but no longer afraid of this
man. 'Ribbons.' *In her hair. In her pointe shoes.*

'Twirling.' I look at him. He nods. 'She loved to dance.' I smile. She did. She does.

The little girl with the ribbons in her hair and the freckles on her nose slips a dainty hand into her father's. 'My Eliza,' he whispers.

Eliza glows as if lit by her very own sun, gossamer-light threads of gleaming mist cloaking her tiny frame. I close my eyes as the light becomes too bright, and when I open them again she has gone.

'Is she . . . still here?' he asks. He looks crestfallen when I shake my head. 'She passed three days ago, I thought –'

'She was looking out for you,' I say. 'It made her . . . forget to let go. It happens sometimes.' I touch his arm again. The roar inside him has quietened. 'Get back to your family. It's they who need you now. And try to think of it as a good thing she's no longer out here with us on the street. It means she's gone where she's supposed to be. She must have been happy.'

He nods, reaches into his pocket and throws some coins into the ragged boy's upturned cap. 'That's all I needed to know,' he says. 'Good day, miss.'

Slumping against the alley wall, I slip my glove back on and press my forehead to the cold, slick stone. Moss tickles my cheek and tiredness throws a weighted blanket round my shoulders. I close my eyes, ignoring questions and the occasional insult from the crowd, that's now thankfully clearing. I open an eye. A couple of schoolboys remain, although I notice they are further back than they were. 'Boo!' I say; they move a little further away, snickering. I shut my eye again, too tired to care.

'You heard what she said.'

My eyes snap open. *Wilf.* I'm so pleased to see him I could sob.

'BOO!' he snarls, stamping a foot in the schoolboys' direction, and they scatter like ants.

'And you,' he says to the little raggedy lad and flicks a coin in the air, 'go on, skedaddle!'

'Cheers, mister!' the boy says, catching the coin and biting it, as if checking for gold. He tips his head to one side. 'Seriously though, what were all tha' about?'

I shake my head. 'Nothing.'

'Oh no, that defin'ly weren't *nothin'*, miss.'

Before I can reply I hear a shout –

'Oi, you mangy little peanut!'

*Whoosh!* I duck as a policeman's baton sings by my ear. '*You* again!' he growls, looking from me to Wilf, to the boy, and back again, wondering which of us to chase.

The boy gives Wilf and me the briefest of nods, kicks the policeman in his shin, then legs it up the street, forcing the policeman to give chase.

## 19

'Why – would anyone – pretend – to – be – a whisperling?' I say between puffs.

Wilf drags me through a maze of tiny back alleys, where scruffy children with bare feet and dirty faces collect water from a hand-pumped well. A boy, no more than four or five, pulls a screaming baby behind him in a packing box with wooden wheels, bouncing the child violently over the cobbles. My hand curls round the coins in my pocket.

'In 'ere,' says Wilf, ducking into a small courtyard about the size of the garden at the pub. It's edged by rows of terraced houses and, on one side, there's a low, brick-built scullery and communal privy, door swinging off its hinges. Lines of damp, droopy washing zig-zag from wall to wall, and I hide behind this miserable bunting until Wilf tells me the coast is clear.

'I'm so sorry,' I say, when we have time to catch our breath. 'Lemon's alive. I know you didn't hurt 'er.'

'Yeah, well.' He shakes his head. 'It must've bin weird finding 'er hair like that.'

'Why did you have it?' He may not have hurt her, but he knows more than he's letting on. 'And why didn't you know I wasn't 'er when we first met? My hair is long.'

'She cut it on the boat. I swept it up but some of it must've gone down the gaps in the boards. And when I first met you, you were wearing a hat.'

This makes perfect sense. 'But why did she want it cut?'

'You'll have to ask 'er when you find 'er. I don't ask questions, ain't none of my business.'

I narrow my eyes. 'So you gave 'er a lift to Gloucester?'

'I thought that was pretty obvious.'

'Well, yes, I suppose it is, now you've told me.'

My fingers stiffen, claw-shaped in annoyance. Boys are *so* irritating.

'Orla – me sister – will let you stay at 'ers tonight, I'm sure of it,' says Wilf. 'It's a bit bigger than the boat, at least.'

'I think I remember your mam,' I say, suddenly. 'She could steer the boat and crochet at the same time.' I can see her sitting by the tiller with her hook and cotton thread, her fingers working nimbly to dip her hook in and out, in and out, round after round, making pretty, lacy mats and doilies that she either sold or used to decorate the cabin.

He looks at me and raises an eyebrow. 'That's right,' he says, smiling. I notice a tiny scar above his lip. 'But it wasn't always like that. We had no money, the boat was tiny and there was no lav. I slept on a mat on the floor and one winter the water froze around us and I had icicles on my nose-drippers.'

'Sorry,' I say. I'm such an idiot. Of course life on a narrowboat wasn't as enchanting as I remember.

A couple of kids come into the courtyard and I freeze, then immediately feel guilty. There are poor people in our village, but somehow the poverty gets hidden among the fields and the cows and the barefooted freedom of the countryside. Just because someone is poor, it doesn't mean they're bad. These children are no different. Yes, it's a dirtier sort of hardship in the city, but that doesn't mean –

*Oof!*

Arms grab at me, scrabbling through my cape and pockets, and there is shouting and '*NO!*' I yell, just before my head hits the cobbles and everything goes black.

When I come to, I'm in a tiny sitting room on a threadbare armchair. A waft of smelling salts hits the back of my throat and I cough.

'Wh-what happened?' My ears buzz and I blink away double vision. I put a hand to my forehead. 'Ouch!' There is a lump, tender and tingling, above my eyebrow and my tummy feels like I've been punched.

'I'm sorry, Nin,' says Wilf. He pops the cork back into the glass container and puts the salts on the mantelpiece. 'There's some bad 'uns round 'ere, little toerags. I'll sort 'em out when I get a chance, don't you worry.'

'He carried you in like a fireman.' A small child, a girl at least a head shorter than me, unseasonably dressed in a white sundress, printed with flowers and tied at the shoulders, points to my spectacles on a sideboard. 'Your glasses aren't broken. They're filthy, though. I'll give 'em a rub if you like.' She shows me a smudge on her belly. 'On a cleaner bit than that,' she giggles.

I pick my glasses up and put them on. At least the fireman's lift explains the ache in my stomach. Thank goodness it's not my lady time; that's the last thing I need.

The little girl smiles. 'They suit you. What's your name?'

'Uh . . . Nin. Nin Esmond. That's just a nickname. It's Violet, officially.'

'I'm Mabel. That there's my uncle. He's called Wilf.'

Wilf hands me a tea in a handle-less enamel cup. His nails are lined with dirt and I hesitate, but my mouth feels like it's been stuffed with rags so I take it and gulp it down greedily. It is delicious: hot and sweet, made with condensed milk.

'Good to know,' he says. He bows theatrically. 'Pleased to re-make your acquaintance, Lady Violet, *officially.*'

I giggle. 'Nin will do fine, thanks. I'm less formal when I'm away from my mansion.'

Wilf throws his head back and laughs. It's so unexpected, I have to blink back a tear. 'So why *Nin*, Nin? What's the story there?' He taps the end of his nose with a finger, as if trying to remember something. His eyes are the same colour as Badger's, like chocolate coins or wet pennies. They're as deep as the sea with sadness, but now, here, there's a sparkle. 'Oh yes! Yer sister said it's because you're a ninny.'

'Well, she would, wouldn't she.' Even when I'm desperately worried about her, my sister can be really annoying. 'Whisperlings have a sort of shine that other whisperlings can see. Not all of us have an eye for it, but me and my sister could always see it in each other, and so could Mam. She said we were "shiny", which Lemon pronounced "niney", and over time "niney" became "Nin" and it sort of stuck.'

'If you say so,' he says with a wink and I glare back at him, but I'm not really annoyed. It's nice to see him so relaxed.

I glance around the little room. OK, so it's not massive – not much bigger than our kitchen – but why doesn't he just stay put with his sister, instead of hopping between here and the boat and sleeping rough in the wood?

'How many of you live here? Your sister and her . . .' I hesitate, aware that if there *was* a husband, there may not be one any more, thanks to the war.

'Husband? Yeah, it's Orla, Reggie and the kids living here.'

'Oh well, that's not too bad. You hear stories about overcrowding and all sorts –'

'And the baby. She sleeps in the drawer.'

*Oh.*

'And then in the *other* bedroom – well, it's the same room, sort of, but there *is* a curtain – there's Maura, Poppy and Gertie.'

'But . . .' I look upwards. 'What about upstairs?'

'Another family live up there.'

So many people, in this tiny space, and that's without Wilf. Little wonder he doesn't stay here permanently.

'Miss, why you wearin' so many clothes?'

I didn't think I was, although compared to Mabel's one item, maybe I am. Under my cape I'm wearing my usual outfit of ankle boots, black knitted stockings, pinafore and woollen roll-neck top, which looks like a fisherman's tunic. I like it because it has two roomy pockets, as does my dress, and you can never have too many pockets, in my book.

'I . . . I didn't have a bag big enough, so I wore as much as I could.' This seems to satisfy Mabel and she wanders away to the corner of the room, fiddling absent-mindedly with the hem of her thin cotton dress.

'Good,' she mutters, ''cuz them bigger boys nicked yer knapsack.'

My heart sinks. It hadn't occurred to me that I'd been robbed, although what other reason would there be for the attack? *And oh no, the ginger cake!* On cue my stomach growls. For some reason, the thought of those horrid thieves eating Mam's spicy loaf annoys me more than anything else.

Wilf looks at me, his expression serious. 'Yer money. They got that too.'

'What?' I slap a hand to my forehead and let out a groan.

'Sorry, Nin. There are bad 'uns around, but we ain't all like that.'

'It's not your fault. Did you see who it was?'

He shakes his head. 'Troublemakers. Parents too busy or too dead to keep 'em in line.'

'They should join the war, like you did. Though Mammy said we should've grabbed Wilf by the legs and not let him go,' says Mabel. I look from him to her and back again. She puts both hands over her mouth, squishing them tight in case more words pop out.

I still can't believe Wilf went to the front. I take a proper look at him, with his shock of sandy hair, wavy like the fronds of an anemone in a rock pool, and thick enough to add two inches to his height. Yes, he's tall, but he's still obviously a *boy*, not yet fixed into the solid shape of a man.

'It was amazin', by the way,' he says quietly.

'What was amazing?'

'The thing you did, back there. I've never seen nothin' like it. It were more than you and your sister did at that messagin', and I've never seen no music hall clairvoyant do —'

'Clairvoyants are *not* whisperlings,' I interrupt, bristling. 'Mediums, psychics, whatever you want to call them — they're con artists, nothing but —'

'OK, OK — I'm sorry!' Wilf puts his hands up as if surrendering. 'Dunno why I was confused, what with so many of you doing the same thing but calling it by a million different names.'

I open my mouth to retort and then shut it when I see Wilf's cheek dimple. He's teasing me. 'All right,' I concede with a shrug, 'I suppose it *is* confusing. But clairvoyants and the like . . . that's a performance for money. And whisperlings . . . that's what we *are*. All of the time.'

He nods his head thoughtfully and taps his regimental badge. 'By your deeds you are known,' he says with a shy smile, modifying the Glosters' motto. He hesitates, and shifts from his position on the floor next to a now sleeping Mabel. 'I saw you take yer glove off. Before you put yer hand on tha' man. I get it now, I think. How they keep you safe.'

I look down at my hands, remembering how I found my gloves on my pillow one day, not long after the rift. Black leather, dainty and ladylike, fastened at the inner wrist with a tiny loop and button. They were left there by my sister, who has only ever wanted to help. I swallow down salty tears. 'And . . . moving about keeps *you* safe?'

He shrugs.

'Safe from what, though?'

'It's best you don't know,' he replies, face grim.

'Well, now I *really* want to know!'

But he won't be drawn any further about that, and so I change the subject. 'I hope he got away from that poxy rozzer,' I say, thinking about the boy from earlier. 'It's so risky, what he's doing.' Getting himself arrested would have been the least of his worries. If things had gone differently he'd have been picking bits of himself off every wall in Gloucester.

Wilf scoffs. 'Risky? Everything's *risky*, Nin. It's risky for me to be in Gloucester, but I 'ave to be 'ere to earn money or I'd end up in the workhouse. I sell papers on the street an' get a shift at the factory when I can.' His eyes flash with anger. 'Me, that kid pretending to be a whisperling, we're *all* desperate. But it's either tha' or starve.' He scrubs at his eyes with the back of his hand and leaves a dark streak of dirt on his face. 'My God, *I'd* pretend to be a whisperling if it put food on the table!'

'But . . . But,' I dither, unsettled by his anger. 'But they might mark *your* house with a C for "Creeper" too?'

Wilf sucks in his cheeks, shaking his head as if dealing with a naive new Tommy, boots clean of blood and mud. He removes one hand from under the sleeping Mabel to gesture around the tiny, damp cottage. 'Look around, Nin. Even if they did, how could it possibly make things worse for people who live like we do?' As he flicks an arm dismissively, two silver half-crowns fall out of his sleeve.

I look at his face. He's horrified; there's no question it's *my* money and *he* took it. My heart plummets. 'Oh, *Wilf*,' I say, tears already falling.

'I . . . I'm sorry, Nin.' His face is ashen. 'It fell out of yer pocket and I picked it up so them other lads wouldn't get it, but then I . . . then I . . .' He shakes his head. 'There's no excuse. I'm so sorry.'

'I trusted you!' My voice is thick and claggy with tears. 'I thought you were my friend, but you're just a rotten . . . *thief*!' I yell, pushing him aside and storming out of the house.

21

Gloucester is laid out like a compass, and the meeting point of its four main streets – Northgate, Southgate, Westgate and Eastgate – is referred to as The Cross. A woman with curling rags in her hair shows me the quickest way to it, and soon I'm back in the main bustle of the city. She warned me not to linger past dark and to 'keep a hand on yer ha'pennies', which was thoughtful if useless advice, given I've already had my money pinched.

The weather has turned. A light, drifting drizzle mists the city and I put up my hood. As I scurry past one of the many black-and-white buildings dotted along the street, my hands prickle, like I'm being poked by a thousand needles. I don't understand the feeling, but I *do* know this place.

Legend has it an old Tudor priest stayed here the night before his execution. We learned about it in school and the details of his burning quickly became a favourite scary story, especially the bit where, as he melted with the flames, he beat at his chest so hard his arm fell off.

I shiver. The thrum of the house's old bones is almost palpable. The frontage is split into two, a sweetshop and a funeral director's business. A granite memorial vase filled with lilies sits in a corner of the undertaker's window. Next to it is a military cap decorated with the gleaming regimental badge of the Glorious Glosters; their distinctive sphynx emblem sits neatly on a pair of white gloves. I lift my glasses to scrub the tears from my eyes – sad for all those soldiers, those boys; sad and angry at Wilf; sad for me.

*Thud, thud, thud.*

'Where's that coming from?' I murmur, pushing my hands against my ears, but it's still there.

*Thud, thud, thud.*

*Trudge, trudge, trudge.*

Marching. It's the sound of marching. I press my nose to the window. Are there soldiers in there? A net curtain hangs behind the window display but I can dimly make out the shop beyond. There's nothing I can see in there that would explain the noise. A frazzled-looking man in an old-fashioned tailcoat counts coffins stacked as high as the ceiling, shaking his head before making a note with a pencil. Maybe he can't keep up with demand. And it isn't just the war. The newspapers report that the Spanish flu has killed as many as died from enemy bullets and my heart squeezes as I think of Mam, poorly back home.

The cathedral bells strike five.

*Wait –*

I turn from the window, push my smeary specs to my forehead and peer through the worsening rain. A woman clutches the lapels of her mac together against the downpour and scurries over the slick cobbles. She isn't alone. A man, young and uniformed and almost transparent, trails behind her as if attached by string. He stretches an arm out to her, but he can't reach her, not quite.

It isn't just him.

*They're everywhere.*

How did I not see them before? My heart hammers in my chest. Trailing behind almost every man, woman and child is a ghost in uniform. So many losses – thousands from Gloucester alone. So many displaced souls.

A young woman pushing a pram stops to adjust its rain-cover. Can she feel him, the dead soldier standing next to her? She looks to me and smiles, but sadness rolls off her and the weight of it pushes me back, pinning me to the window. The whole city is grieving.

Suddenly among the crowds I catch sight of that horrible strawberry-faced policeman. I can't let him see me. I drag myself away from the window, pull my hood up and walk briskly away. After I've gone a short distance I duck into an alleyway, keeping an eye on him until he's safely out of sight.

There's a pub, The Bull, about halfway down the passage and I take cover under its jutting eaves to shake the rain from my cape and wipe my specs. The hum of chatter and wafts of cigarette smoke and beer fumes creep from under the door, reminding me of the smell of home. A movement catches my eye, like the judder of a film catching on the cinema reel. I gingerly put my glasses back on. Not a handshake away from me a shadow skins from the wall, slowly gaining shape like plaster being poured into a mould. It flexes and forms until it's a young woman in a brown smock and mob cap. I spy a raised welt on her neck.

'I din' do it!' she says as she loops round me. 'They said I did, but I din'. They knew it, too, but din' say so till after I swung.'

The roar and heckle of a bloodthirsty ancient crowd echoes through the alley, and she glides by me, smiling a black-toothed smile, her head at a disturbing angle. My heart thuds.

And then a small, cold hand covers my mouth and pulls me into the shadows.

'Was that Mary again?' says a girl, shorter than me and blonde-haired. Her curls peek from a boyish cap and frame a face as round and shiny and blue-eyed as a china doll's.

'Mary?'

'You know, hung for a crime she didn't commit? Goes on and on and on about it.' The girl sniffs and wipes her nose with the back of her hand. 'Bit boring, really.' She smiles and her face blooms, making my heart give a little jump. 'Change the bleedin' record, Mary, love!' She giggles, making herself laugh. 'Though I'm glad she caught your eye, cos I've been looking all over for you.'

The girl is wearing a uniform of sorts, and frowns at me, like an angry, trouser-wearing Girl Guide. 'Where the heck 'ave you been, any road?' She looks me up and down, and plucks at my cape. 'Better,' she says. 'More practical.' She tips her head and pokes my glasses with a finger. 'Nice touch,' she says approvingly.

'You're a whisperling,' I say. The faintest glow radiates from under her cap, like there's a torch under there.

She peers at me like I'm a specimen in a jar. ''Ave you had a knock to the head?'

'I have, as it happens,' I reply honestly, moving my hood up a touch so she can see the lump on my forehead.

'Ooh, that's nasty! Who did that?' She rolls up her sleeves and sticks her head out of the alleyway, looking left and right. 'I'll 'ave 'em for yer, you know I will.'

I don't doubt it. 'No, there's no need, really. It was a while ago and they've long gone.'

'Right, come on then, we'd better get back. Maeve'll stick some herbal balm on that for yer. Sort it right out.'

'Maeve McQueen?' Excitement bubbles in my tummy. 'From the newspaper!' I tap my cape pocket.

I brought the cutting with me, for information purposes only. Not because I've studied it every night, imagining what it would be like to be friends with them. 'And you're Florence Redfern!' Recognition slots into place like a puzzle piece. Her picture is also in the newspaper article, although the one they've chosen makes her look angry and threatening –

Florence Redfern: A troubled girl who brought the good name of the Girl Guides into disrepute . . .

What on earth did she actually do?

Florence looks at me like I have two heads. 'Right, that's it. Let's get you back.' It's obvious she thinks I'm Lemon, which means that my sister must be close by – perhaps even wherever Florence is taking me. This is going to be easier than I thought!

Suddenly, she slaps a hand to my mouth and flattens both of us to the wall.

'Hey! Wha' d'you think you're doin'?' She squishes my lips between her finger and thumb. '*Ow!* Stobbit!'

Florence puts a finger to her lips. Light shimmers across the entrance to the alleyway and immediately

I know that it's her: that lovely, shining whisperling girl in the mossy-green cape from before. Gleaming like a fallen sunray, she glides past us like a bride and I reach an arm out to grab her. Florence pulls my arm back and shakes her head.

'What you doing, you twit?' she snaps.

I look back at the girl. Surely we can't be hiding from *her*?

'Right,' says Florence, releasing me. 'That were lucky. She's bad news, she is. Proper wrong 'un.' She wipes her fingers on her trousers and gestures at me to follow her as she trots down the alley, away from town.

My heart stretches like a rubber band. Who should I trust? That whisperling girl, with her soft, kind voice and gentle manner, and her incredible, other-worldly glow, or − I rub at my mouth − this scrappy, bossy girl with the pinching fingers, who the newspaper says is trouble? I'm not given a choice; Florence stomps furiously towards me, scolds me for 'dilly-dallying', grabs my arm and drags me away.

I follow her at pace, through the alleyway, across a road and then towards the docks, the skeletal arches of the remains of Blackfriars Priory on our left. 'Come on!' she yips impatiently and for a moment I'm reminded of Badger and that insistent terrier way of his. 'You know we shouldn't be out like this in the daytime!' I look round, to see if we're being followed, and when I turn back she's gone.

I spin on the spot. She's completely disappeared! *Was she a ghost?* No, it isn't possible. She was solid and –

'Hey!' A hand waves up at me from beside a weathered tombstone. I jump back in horror. Oh my goodness, is she one of the *undead*? 'What are you waiting for? Come *onnnn*!' Florence's head emerges, hands pushing up the metal grill that's covering whatever it is she's standing in. She glares at me from behind the bars, as if she's in prison, and, without another word, I follow her into the black mouth of the tunnel.

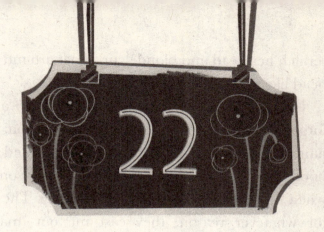

22

The tunnel is lit by burning torches dotted every hundred yards or so, with knee-height arrows in chalk at similar intervals, showing the way. The walls are gently curved, and as we walk I trail my fingers along them; even under my gloves I can feel the change in textures, slick and mossy in places, dry and rough in others. Every so often, the trunk of the tunnel breaks off into branches of differing sizes, some barely wider than me. I shudder, not wanting to imagine what it would be like in those tight little wormholes. I tug at the neck of my tunic, feeling claustrophobic. It would be very easy to get lost down here.

'How long has this been here?' I ask.

'Did you not get all of this information in your orientation?' says Florence. She takes her cap off to scratch her head and blonde curls float around her head like soap bubbles.

'Oh, you know me,' I say nervously, 'I'm a bit forgetful.' It's obvious she thinks I'm Lemon; my hair is tucked into the back of my cape and my hood is up, so why wouldn't she? I decide to confess when we reach wherever it is we're going. Then if, for whatever reason, they cast me out (maybe Lemon has told them that it's my fault she ran off . . .), I'll go and find that lovely, graceful whisperling girl.

'Well,' she replies, brightening, 'it's lucky it was me who came to find you, wasn't it? Flo Redfern never misses an opportunity for a bit of tunnel-ology.'

'Tunnel-ology?'

'Yes. The study of tunnels.' She is completely straight-faced and then collapses in laughter. 'Oh mate, the look on your chops!'

We come to a chunky wooden door which reaches to my nose. Flo knocks, three times slowly, and then five times quickly, which must be some sort of code. There is a flick of a latch, and the door opens. Flo peeks through, squinting. 'After you,' she says with a thumbs up.

It's dark down here, but I put my thumbs up in reply, as I guess Lemon would, take a big, confident stride and boldly step through.

The last thing I hear is Flo's horrified shriek as I tumble down into the dark.

I'm on my back, the fall broken by a mound of blankets over what I assume to be soft soil.

'Are you all right?' says a girl with an American accent.

'Is she alive, is she alive, is she alive?' Flo jumps to the ground and kneels beside me, the rope and slat ladder I was *supposed* to climb down swinging in and out of my eyeline. An open-mouthed girl holding a long, wooden pole looks from the raised opening towards me and back again. She adjusts her baker-boy cap and pushes the rod against the door, as though spearing a dragon. It shuts with a satisfying *clunk*.

Lights bloom in my vision. My glasses were knocked off in the fall; someone passes them to me and I put them on. I squeeze my eyes shut and open them again, but the lights are still there. Is it the candles? But then I realize: I'm surrounded by faces, like a mouse in a ring of meercats. The glow wasn't so fierce when Flo was on her own, but here, together, the effect is spellbinding. The shine is coming from them.

'You're *all* whisperlings?' I venture.

'We sure are,' says the American girl. Her very white teeth are laced with metal and her hair is plaited close to her head in what looks like a hundred braids that fall almost to her waist. Some are dotted with tiny gold cuffs. Her skin is brown and her nose is pierced with a dainty silver stud. I'm so captivated I can barely breathe. 'And you are *not* Clemency.' She gestures to Flo, who helps me to a sitting position. 'Flo, seriously, how did you not realize?'

Another girl, the one in the baker-boy cap, catches a skein of my hair in her hand and waggles it at Flo, like my hair is a paintbrush and she's a canvas. 'Good spot, Sherlock,' she teases.

Flo is bent double with her hands on her knees, breathing heavily. 'It was – tucked – in her – cape,' she says, panting. 'And, er . . . maybe because,' she says, lifting a hand and circling it at my face, 'maybe because, apart from the glasses – which, by the way, I thought were a cunning disguise – they look *exactly* the same.'

*And maybe because you were too busy telling me off*, I think, but this isn't the time to find fault. I look around instead.

I've landed in some sort of barrel-shaped, medieval cellar, with a low, arched ceiling and squat, ancient-looking columns that I reckon have been there since Roman times. A recess in one wall looks like it's acting as larder; it even has a chicken-wire door. From other neat little nooks, candles scatter light, and on a stubby little cast-iron stove a kettle sputters and pops. A low tomb-like structure is covered with a tablecloth and laid with blue-rimmed enamel cups and plates. In one recess is a bookshelf, in another a pile of neatly folded towels. An ancient-looking stone trough is partly shielded by a screen . . . Could that be a *bath*? Excitement bubbles up from my tummy. The mams would *love* it down here. It's like a cross between an ancient crypt and a fairy grotto.

'You like it?' asks the American girl and I nod. It's *beautiful*. I could clap my hands and spin, giddily. 'When you're feeling a little better, we'll show you around. But in the meantime,' she says, 'my name is Jessie. This here is Flo – you've met her already – and those other two are Velvet and Maeve.'

I smile, suddenly shy. 'I'm Violet – Nin for short. Not short for "Violet", obviously, but –'

'Yeah, it's OK. Clemency told us. Hello, Nin,' says Jessie with a smile. 'Welcome to the Creeper Gang.'

## 23

'The *Creeper* Gang?' I flinch at the old insult.

'We're reclaiming it,' asserts Jessie. 'It's kinda cool, don't you think?' She notes my blank expression. 'You know, cool? Um . . . you'd say *nifty*, I guess?'

'Er, yes, I suppose so. *Cool*.' I like the way it feels to say it. It reminds me of when I first saw Bessie in her wide-leg trousers.

'So, you're here to find Clemency?' She has a slight lisp, presumably from the strange metal on her teeth.

'Yes!' I've been so entranced by the grotto and these girls that I'd almost forgotten I'm supposed to be looking for my sister. 'Is Lemon staying with you?' I ask, suddenly frantic. 'I thought she was just sulking, then missing, then *dead*.' I pause. 'Oh no! The mams still think she is!' I jump up to leave. 'I have to tell them, I have to . . . Oh dear –' I woozily sit back down – 'I don't feel too well.'

'That'll happen when you fall on your head.' A girl wearing a blush-pink fringed kimono over a pair of denim jeans (*Jeans!* Like a cowboy!) passes me a glass of water. 'Here, drink this.' About a dozen thin, silver bangles tinkle as she flutters a hand in greeting. 'I'm Velvet.' She peers at me. 'Sorry, that's so rude of me. But you really are identical. It's kind of magical.'

Velvet . . . Ravenscroft? The name Ravenscroft was mentioned in the newspaper but their name wasn't Velvet. It was a boy's name and the article said they were a 'trickster', only pretending to be a girl. That doesn't match the elegant, sparky girl before me. I realize with a start that I'm staring at her like at a painting in a museum. She frowns at me and, face burning, I look away. 'I saw your picture, Velvet,' I say, muttering towards the floor, 'in the newspaper. With the other missing girls. I could tell you were all whisperlings, from the glow.'

'You can see the whisperling glow in a photograph?'

I smile sheepishly and Velvet whistles through her teeth. 'Wow, that's amazing! I can only see it in person, just about.' She lowers her voice to a whisper. 'Between you and me, I'm not sure Flo can see it at all.' She raises an eyebrow at me. 'I thought it was one of those things that develops as your skills get stronger. You must be a pretty powerful whisperling.'

I blush. 'I don't know about that.' I reach into my pocket to show her the article, which she scans briefly before passing it back with a dismissive shrug. I tuck the paper back in my pocket, feeling foolish. Velvet is a girl, no doubt about that.

I clear my throat, which feels claggy with awkwardness. 'Is my sister all right?' I ask.

Jessie crouches in front of me. She wears a cut-off military jacket and flannel trousers tucked into chunky, thick-soled boots. Maybe I'm imagining things, but for a second it looks like Jessie flickers in and out of focus. 'Clemency is staying with us and I'm sure she'll be back later.'

'You don't *sound* sure,' I say, looking round at the others.

Flo snorts. 'Keeping tabs on that one is a full-time job. Like nailing jelly to the wall,' she mutters.

'Flo!' scolds Jessie. Then she turns to me. 'Your sister is fine. She's brave and loyal and, yes, sometimes she can make rash decisions.' She smiles. 'But I guess you already know that. And there's something else you should know,' she continues, chewing her lip. 'I . . . I don't think Clemmy was expecting you to come find her.' She tips her head to one side. 'And what's with the name "Lemon"? Why do you call Clemmy that?'

So she's *Clemmy* here, is she? *Yuck*. The warm-custard feeling of relief at finding out my sister's alive is curdled. 'We call her Lemon on account of her sourness,' I say, which isn't true at all. It's because 'Lemon' was easier for little me to say than 'Clemency', and Mam thought it was cute.

'I kinda like it,' says Jessie with a grin. 'Oh! And I'm sorry if this sounds obvious –' she suddenly sounds serious – 'but I have to say it to everyone, from the minute you join us. Makes me feel antsy if I don't.'

I don't know what 'antsy' means but it sounds itchy.

'The first rule of the Creeper Gang is that you can't tell anyone about us. Not a soul. No one.'

I nod. It's an easy rule to keep. Who would I tell? Lemon is pretty much my only friend. I look round at the eclectic group and feel a rush of jealousy. *But Lemon's got these new friends now who have replaced me.* My tummy feels heavy and empty at the same time. 'It's all right,' I say, thinking of how Lemon slammed the door in my face when I tried to connect to her. 'I know she doesn't want me here cramping her style.'

'What?' says Maeve, pulling her hat off. Red hair tumbles to her knees like Rapunzel, and she rolls it back up and piles it on her head, shoving two pencils from her pocket through to secure it. It looks like knitting needles in a ball of wool. ' "Cramping her style"? No, Nin, that's not it at all.'

'So why is she trying so hard to keep me from finding 'er?' I'm on the edge of tears. 'She's my twin, we're supposed to have a connection. I tried to contact her –'

'You tried to *what*?' Flo interrupts, narrowing her eyes at me. 'Hang on –' She rummages in her pockets, brings out a notepad and pencil, and crosses her legs. 'How would that work, exactly?' She taps her bottom lip with the pencil, the pad resting on her knees.

'It's hard to explain. I found 'er ponytail . . .' I pause, distracted by the sound of Flo's pencil scribbling on paper. 'Sorry, what are you doing?'

Flo looks up. 'Making notes,' she says, like it's the most obvious thing in the world. She waves the pencil at me. 'So, go on. You found her hair . . .'

I look to Jessie, bewildered, and she puts a hand on Flo's shoulder. It barely touches her, but it's enough for Flo to lower her notepad. 'We want to document everything,' explains Jessie. 'Sharing stories verbally is a powerful thing, y'know? In some cultures it's the only way history is recorded – passing stories from one generation to the next. But we have to have some way of recording it permanently. So it doesn't get lost.'

' "For those that come after",' I whisper, parroting what Mam told me and Lemon.

'Yes!' says Flo. 'Apparently there's this book –'

I look up. 'The Book of Devona.'

'You know about it?' Jessie smacks her forehead. 'Of course you do! Clemmy knew too. Sorry, I forgot for a second. You guys were its guardians, weren't you? Before it was stolen?'

'Guardians?' I haven't heard it referred to as that. It sounds like we should have taken much more care of it than just keeping it stashed behind the bar. It wasn't even locked, the key to its velvet-lined, wooden box having been lost by a previous 'guardian', years before. I blush, embarrassed. 'So you're making notes,' I say, feeling I'm edging towards understanding, 'in the hope that, what, one day you can add them to the book?'

Flo nods. 'Or start our own book.'

Maeve opens a wooden chest, takes out a sheepskin, shakes it and puts it on the floor to sit on. 'So I guess if you've heard of the book, it's fair to assume you've heard of The Righteous, too?'

I nod. A thought strikes me. 'You knew about the book and The Righteous before Clem–' I shake my head – 'before *Lemon* met up with you?'

'That's right,' says Flo, eyes dancing. 'Ask us how,' she says, jittering in her seat. 'Go on, ask us how!'

'Very well.' I smile, playing along. 'How?'

'*They* told us.' She gestures around, as if introducing a performer to the stage. 'Do you see them too?'

Yes, I see them.

Shimmering shapes of gilded mist shifting in and out of focus, wafting peacefully around the grotto. Some wispy and see-through, others as fully formed and detailed as me. A woman in a long white tunic, her hair blooming around her head like seafoam, trails her fingers along the walls as if reminiscing about her time here; another woman, white-haired and brittle-looking, accompanied by a skinny black ghost cat winding in and out of her legs, sniffs the air above the pot and pulls a face, unimpressed. She looks over at me and gives me a wink, which is so unexpected it makes me giggle.

So, yes, I *do* see them. And they are beautiful.

24

To me, ghosts are a bit like birds. I know it's odd, but it's sort of how I think of them. Imagine a bird choosing *you* to perch on, just for a moment, before it flutters away to wherever it's off to. How exciting would that be! How thrilling! A beautiful thing. But if that one bird became two, then ten, then a hundred birds, flapping and pecking and squawking . . . well. My beautiful, fluttering birds turn into a wake of vultures pecking at carrion, pecking at *me*.

But this . . . this is incredible.

'You can *all* see them?' I ask, astonished.

'Yup,' says Flo with the pride of a child who has won a prize at school. 'Isn't it *great*?'

'Actually, yes, it really is!'

The girls gather closer. 'This is so cool,' says

Jessie, using that strange word again. 'These guys,' she says, gesturing to the glinting ghosts, 'are all *whisperling* spirits. And our being able to see them so clearly . . . it must be something to do with being here together in this place.'

And *this place* is remarkable. After a bit of a sit-down it's decided I'm recovered enough for a tour. Arm linked in mine, Velvet shows me around, pointing out details as if we're browsing for groceries at market. She tells me of how here, under the city of Gloucester, lies a secret: a scattering of ancient catacombs, cellars and vaults, threaded together by a web of tunnels and burrows. 'And here,' she says, pointing up towards a copper pipe poking out high up on the wall, 'an air tube. So we don't suffocate,' she adds, cheerfully.

'Did you do that?'

'Do I look like a plumber?' she says, dropping my arm so she can twirl like a ballerina on a musical box. The fringe on her kimono flutters out like butterfly wings. 'No, it's been there for years.' She squints. 'You can tell by the rusty trickle.'

'Who put it there?' I ask, but she doesn't know. None of them do. I look round the grotto, at the various resident whisperling ghosts in clothes that span a museum's worth of ages. This place has been here for decades. Centuries, even. 'Where do they come out, the breathing tubes?'

'That's a good question,' says Maeve, stirring a pot of delicious-smelling soup in what can only be described as a cauldron. 'We know where one or two are, but whoever originally created this place understood the need to be discreet. The tubes are practically invisible at street level.' She points to a flue which disappears into the wall. 'No idea where that one goes. It must be attached to a chimney somewhere, but –' She shrugs.

I look up to the vaulted ceiling. 'So you don't know what's directly above us?'

'Not a clue.'

I think for a moment. The girls have added bits and pieces to the cellar; the tea lights and household linens and food, but the bones of this place have been here for years. 'Whisperlings have been hiding forever,' I say, mainly to myself, although I'm sure the ghost with the cat also nods in agreement. All of these bright, intuitive, remarkable girls and women, having to hide away because . . . because *why*? Because we're misunderstood? Because people are fearful of us or jealous of our gifts? Because we're *women*?

'All of these ghosts must have hidden down here at some point,' I say, just knowing. My tummy flips with sudden excitement. 'Have you spoken to *all* of them?' The grotto with all its whisperling ghosts is like a real-life version of the Book of Devona. 'Think of what we could learn!'

Jessie appears at Maeve's side. 'Looks good,' she says, peering into the bubbling soup.

'It's ready to eat,' says Maeve. 'Dinner's up, everyone!'

As we queue for supper, Jessie answers my question. 'They're a great resource,' she says, 'our resident ghosts, but they only know what they *knew*, if you get what I mean.'

I think I do. 'You mean, they only have knowledge of what happened in their own lifetime?'

'Exactly that,' she confirms, and I feel very pleased with myself. 'They can each tell us what happened to them, but they can't scoot off and find out where the other missing girls are, or any other useful information.'

The missing girls. So there are more! I'd hoped the four members of the Creeper Gang and Lemon were the only ones.

We circle back to a low tombstone laid for tea

and sit cross-legged on a warm, fluffy sheepskin to eat. The soup is delicious, and as soon as I finish I could eat it all over again. Velvet collects our bowls to be washed up. There's a rota, apparently. I wonder if I'll be here long enough to be added to it.

'Agnes can be chatty,' says Velvet. 'Her cat, not so much.' She smiles and waggles her fingers towards the white-haired ghost who winked at me. She shakes her head in response. 'Agnes told us about the Book of Devona, and how in her time one of The Righteous tried to have a young girl executed for a crime she didn't commit.'

A chill runs down my spine. I know that story. 'Mam knows a whisperling who stood up to The Righteous. It was twenty-odd years ago, but –'

'Was it Peggy? Peggy Devona?' Maeve's eyes shine with excitement.

My jaw drops. '*Yes*, how do you –'

'Oh, wow!' Velvet gasps and clutches her hands to her chest like she's swooning over a movie star. '*The* Peggy Devona!'

Flo shadow-boxes the air and makes *pow-pow* noises.

'She took on a member of The Righteous and won,' says Jessie. 'Her whisperling skills are legendary! Agnes told us. How does your mom know her?'

Blood thuds in my ears. I have a burning need to go home and ask Mam some questions. 'Peggy's my mam's second cousin,' I say quietly. 'We call her Great Aunt Peggy.'

It's like a magical spell has been thrown over the gang. No one says a word. I hear a tiny thread of condensation trickle down a wall of the cavern and splash on to the floor.

Flo discreetly flicks her notepad open. 'You're related to Peggy? You're a *Devona*?'

I shrug. 'I . . . don't know.'

'You don't *know*?'

'My surname is Esmond!'

'But your bloodline is Devona.' Jessie sits back on her haunches and puts her hands to her face. 'This is . . . bad. Why didn't Clemmy tell us this?'

'Bad? Why?'

'Because if The Righteous find out you and your sister are Devonas, and are in Gloucester, they'll be after you, for sure. You guys have history with them. We're going to have to tighten security.' She gestures to the other girls. 'Maeve, Flo, go check the tunnels.

Make sure the seams are properly blocked. We'll have to keep the noise down a bit as well.' She turns to Velvet. 'I'm looking at you. No singing, OK?'

Velvet rolls her eyes. 'You're such a party-pooper.' She grins, and twirls a lock of chestnut-brown hair around a finger. Her nails are painted sky-blue. 'Singing is my thing,' she says, seriously. 'It was the sound of the choristers' singing that drew me to Gloucester.'

'Oh?' That's interesting. 'For me, it was a vision of the cathedral tower. I saw the shape of one of the pinnacles at the top; it looked like a witch's hat.'

'Each of us sensed something different that brought us here. Like a whisperling radar or something,' Jessie explains. 'Maeve had a vision of the docks. Flo could smell the fish and chips from the black-and-white chippy.'

'I love me chips, what can I say?' says Flo with a shrug.

*A whisperling radar.* A weird, magnetic pull, dragging whisperlings to the city.

Velvet sees me looking at her pretty blue nails. 'Lapis-blue oil paint and varnish. Natty, no?'

I smile. It *is* natty.

'This is serious,' says Jessie sharply. The grin falls from Velvet's face.

'Are they likely to try and find me? Us?' I ask.

It's like lighting a touchpaper. 'Yes!' snaps Jessie, smoke-black eyes flashing with anger. 'Why do you think we're hiding? For fun?'

I sink back, face burning.

'Whisperlings are being drawn to the city, but then they disappear. Talk is, The Righteous are after a *particular* whisperling. Why, we don't know. But it would make sense that they're after the best they can get.'

I swallow, feeling all eyes on me.

Jessie moves closer. 'They want a powerful whisperling. Of the original line, maybe. A Devona.'

'Like me?' I whisper.

'Like you,' says Jessie. 'And like your sister.'

'I'm sorry,' says Jessie, later. 'That was out of line. There was no need for me to go off at you like that.'

'No, I get it,' I say. 'You feel responsible for us.'

'I need to show you something,' she says, sputtering out of view. She returns a moment later carrying a folder. 'This is a record of all of the girls who went missing in this – in your – time period. Not just from Gloucester. It's collated from newspaper articles from all over the country.' She carefully takes out a paper, unfolds it and turns it to show me. Dozens of faces stare out from the page, shining like the sun through a kaleidoscope.

'Whisperlings,' I say. 'All of them.'

Jessie nods and refolds the document. When she looks at me, her eyes shine with tears. She lowers her voice. 'Where I'm from, or should I say *when*, the other missing girls . . . we didn't find them. That's why I'm here – to figure out where they are. You four, you were the only survivors.'

*Four?* There must be twenty or more girls on that chart! I'm about to ask more but Jessie flickers in and out of focus again, and I can't put it off any longer.

Jessie is a ghost, quite obviously; at times I can see the wall behind her through her body. But I've seen enough ghosts to know there's something very different about her. 'Who are you?' I ask. A whisperling glow shimmers around her head. 'What? How . . . ?'

'It's complicated,' she says. 'I'm sort of a ghost, I guess. But I don't come from the past. And I'm not dead.'

'Go on, tell her,' urges Flo, tapping her notepad with the pencil.

Jessie glares at her, juddering slightly, perhaps this time in irritation rather than ghostliness. 'I'm from the future,' she says, deadpan.

Flo peals with laughter, and then slaps a hand over her mouth. 'Sorry,' she says. 'But it boggles me every time.'

I can't disagree: it really is boggling. 'If you're from the future,' I say, 'why can't you just tell us what to do? Can't you tell us how to solve this? What happens to us?'

Velvet wiggles on her seat. 'Ask me. I know, I know!' She shoves one arm high in the air, propped up by the other as if answering a question in class. 'There are rules,' she says, mock-seriously. 'Should she tell us anything that unbalances the universal time-bobbins, then all of our heads will explode.' She shrugs. 'Or something.'

Jessie sighs. This is obviously not a new conversation. 'There's a bit more to it than that,' she says, side-eyeing a smirking Velvet, 'but yeah, that's the gist of it. But one thing I *can* tell you, without risk of any head-explosions, is where your sister is.'

Flo slaps a hand to her forehead. 'Of course! It's Thursday! Let's go get Lemon.'

Preparations to leave the grotto to collect Lemon take a boisterous turn. From an enormous trunk that appeared from nowhere, garments are plucked out and paraded and reflections checked in the copper-speckled surface of an old looking glass propped up against a wall. Jessie raises an eyebrow at me and shakes her head like a disapproving governess.

'You said four of us survive,' I say quietly to her over the hubbub. 'You meant five, didn't you? Me, Velvet, Maeve, Flo and Lemon. Five.'

'Oh yes, of course.' She smiles. 'I got it wrong. Math isn't my strong point.'

But I can see from her reflection in the mirror behind her that her fingers are crossed.

25

Outside the entrance to the New Inn, a monkey in a blue-striped waistcoat collects coins as a barrel organ plinks and plonks and toots. He has a chain round his neck and a lead attached to that. Occasionally the little capuchin does a back flip and the crowd applauds, not noticing the organ grinder's sly flick of the wrist.

'I hope he bites him,' says Velvet, adjusting the monocle she chose to wear for no other reason than it looks 'swell'. I nod in agreement, unable to speak. The day has caught up with me and the sight of this poor, badly treated little creature is pushing me close to tears.

But the monkey isn't why we're here. Stepping into the New Inn pub is like stepping on to a stage in Shakespeare's day; as soon as you walk through the entrance, it is like you've travelled back into Elizabethan times. Timbered galleries overlook a central courtyard and you could easily imagine – or in my case see – minstrels peering over a rail, a court jester in a brightly coloured, three-pointed hat, gambolling along the wooden benches, his curled, bell-tipped shoes tinkling as he dances. I look back to the street outside and with some relief hear the clank of trams and see people passing by in modern-day clothing. I'm reassured that we haven't really been whisked away in some sort of time machine.

An aircraft passes overhead, the moan of its engines causing everyone to stop and look skyward, following its path until they almost topple backwards. It's not uncommon to see them pass over – they're built not far from here – but still, seeing the red, white and blue insignia of the Royal Air Force on the underside is a relief. You wouldn't catch me in one of those spindly-looking things. How do they stay up there? Wilf's face flashes into my mind. I hope he didn't hear that one go by.

We slide into a room marked PRIVATE and take a seat at the back. Here, in a small, timber-panelled space, barely lit with the half-glow of rheumy oil lamps, a séance is about to start. An advertising board at the entrance to the pub informed us that Blythe Bumble can *connect the bereaved with their loved ones for half a guinea each!* – and for a fleeting second I wondered if Blythe could be genuine. Perhaps she too was affected by the rift – or 'the shock' or 'the call' . . . Turns out all the girls have a different name for it. But Blythe sits in shadow, preparing for her performance, without even a glow-worm's worth of whisperling shine coming from her. I shake my head, feeling cross. Keeping the lights low so customers can't see what you're up to is a common trick. I should have known it would be a sham.

Flo, Velvet and I are all in disguise. The dressing-up box in the grotto is bountiful, full of hats, coats, dresses, suits and accessories, some extremely old and others bang up to date. I picked out a black feathered fan to hide behind, and a modern, ankle-length, navy-twill skirt to wear under my cape. I feel very grown up indeed and am excited that when we *do* find Lemon, she will be jealous of my outfit.

'Whisperlings *never* try to reach anyone specific,' I whisper to Flo. 'It wouldn't work even if we did. They just aren't going to show up for any ghoulish Glenda clicking 'er fingers. What a crock of –' A woman in the row in front, eyes red-rimmed and glassy, turns to glower at me in disapproval. I flick open my fan to cover my face. Jessie warned me to be careful; she didn't want me coming at all, really, but I insisted.

It used to be a bit of a laugh, this sort of thing, like having your tea-leaves read. I glance about from behind my fan. No one here seems to be having fun, unless your idea of a good night out is weeping quietly into a handkerchief while someone pats your back and says, 'There, there.' I throw my most evil glare at the woman on stage. These people, like those who come to our messagings, just want the chance to say goodbye. How dare she make money from their grief?

'Is there anybody there?' chants Blythe Bumble in a wobbly sort of voice. She is a kindly-looking, squashy sort of woman wearing dark clothes and an old-fashioned black bonnet with frills round the edge. The type who would call you 'dearie' and offer you a butterscotch should you sit next to her on the tram.

'I'm getting . . . a man,' Blythe is saying now, eyes closed, head swaying.

The crowd is quiet, save for bums shuffling on seats and an awkward cough or two.

'In uniform!' At this, there is a murmur of interest. 'Are you a soldier, my spectral friend? Please knock once for yes, twice for no.'

There's a short pause, and then: *knock*.

The audience crackles with excited, nervous chatter. Blythe appeals for calm. 'Something is coming through . . . a letter, perhaps.' She closes her eyes and runs randomly through the alphabet. When she gets to 'the letter J!', a woman in the front row gasps and Blythe's eyes snap open, flicking towards the sound. She gives the tiniest of self-satisfied nods and puts her hands out like she's about to play the piano. On the table in front of her is a collection of items, arranged in a semicircle, and while Blythe wiggles her fingers over them in mid-air, I look to Flo for answers.

'Her assistant gathers keepsakes from folk in the audience beforehand, finds out their meaning, that sort of thing,' explains Flo, quietly. 'She reads people's reactions, that's how she knows which supposed ghost to choose to "speak" with. Watch.'

I cross my arms, scrunch down in my seat and glare at Blythe, extra hard. 'Yes, well, let's see if she can read *my* reaction,' I mutter, adding a scornful snort which I turn into a fake sneeze in case the lady in front hears me again.

'Button!' warbles Blythe, overacting. 'Playing card, *backgammon* –'

There is another intake of breath. Blythe's hand snaps back to the backgammon counter. She focuses her gaze on the woman in the front row who reacted to it.

'Someone enjoyed playing backgammon with you, didn't they, lovely?' The woman in the front row sobs gently; her companion passes her a handkerchief. 'I have him here. Your lovely John . . . James . . . Jim –' she stops guessing as the woman gives a tiny, involuntary nod. 'Jim! Jim is here, lovely. He misses you, he does, but he's fine, he's at peace, he's –'

'NOT HERE!' yells a voice. A figure in the audience wearing a very familiar black gown rises to her feet. 'And even if he was, he wouldn't be talking to *you*, you big fat faker!' My sister shakes a tiny, furious fist in Blythe's direction. I sit up in my seat.

'Not you *again*,' groans Blythe with a strange, pained gurgle.

Velvet gives me a sharp nudge. 'Here we go,' she says with a grin. 'Welcome to the Lemon show.'

As well as the annoyingly gorgeous, gothic-style gown, Lemon is wearing a top hat trimmed with a black lace veil that covers her face. I look down at my neat modern skirt and cuss her under my breath. She looks fabulous.

'I am very sorry for your loss,' says Lemon, giving the woman in the front row a strange little bow, palms together as if in prayer. 'But this woman –' she points at Blythe Bumble – 'is a fraud!'

The clairvoyant's face is as red and snorting as an angry bull. 'Get. Out,' she seethes. 'Get out, get out, get OUT!' Blythe leaps to her feet. The table wobbles and tips, buttons and coins spilling to the floor. Something nudges my foot, and I bob down and pick it up. It's the backgammon counter.

'What's that?' says someone in the crowd. My hand fizzes as I curl my fingers round the counter. But that isn't what they mean.

Around Blythe's waist is a butcher's hook attached to a sturdy leather belt. 'Ah-HA! Exhibit A!' cries Lemon, triumphant. She jabs a finger at the butcher's hook. 'The knocking you all just heard? That's how she does it, by whacking that hook against the underside of the table!'

The room stills. *She's done it*, I think, feeling a rush of pride. But then I look at Flo, who shakes her head and warns me to hold my horses.

'Folk sometimes don't take kindly to having their foolishness pointed out,' she says. 'Especially when the lie is the only hope they've got.'

She's right. The clamour in the room is building up and up, like the agitated whinnying and clattering noise from the stables when a fox is on the prowl. 'Get out of here!' says an angry voice.

'I quite agree,' says Lemon. She pulls herself up to her full height, which isn't very tall, though her new hat adds a few inches. 'Leave this place, fake lady-clairvoyant! You are not welcome here.'

'Not 'er,' says the man, shaking his fist. 'You!'

Lemon deflates like an underbaked meringue. 'What?'

'Oh dear,' says Velvet. 'This can happen sometimes. We'd better get her out of here.' She glides through the crowd to Lemon's side, whips the shawl from her shoulders and wraps it round my sister, firmly guiding her towards the exit. 'There, there,' Velvet says loudly but firmly, as if speaking to a toddler having a tantrum, 'let's get you home.'

'No!' Lemon turns her head to yell again at Blythe Bumble, who is now purple-faced. 'THAT woman is a fraud. These people are being conned. It isn't right! YOU'RE BEING CONNED!'

Velvet and Lemon stop at Flo and me and together we move to follow them out. 'They don't *care*, Clemency.' Velvet sing-speaks through a smile, like a ventriloquist. 'If we don't get you out of here, they're going to *kiiiiill* you. Besides,' she adds, 'you have a visitor.'

Lemon's eyes lock on mine, and if looks could kill, I'd have died once more. But I don't care. She can huff all she likes – which, knowing her, will be a lot. She's alive, and that's all that matters.

'Wait!' I say, a familiar tickle on the back of my neck. There *is* someone here. There are *many* of them here. I slip off my glove and squeeze the backgammon counter between my fingers. I can see him, the ghost of Jim, hovering behind his wife. He looks very handsome in his uniform. He's mouthing something, but I can't quite make it out, so as Lemon passes me I grab her hand.

*Whoosh!*

The light around us flares and shimmers.

'Excuse me,' I say to the tearful lady in the front row. 'Your Jimmy cheated at backgammon, every time. He kept a trick dice in his sock. It had sixes on each side. He thought it was funny.' I can see ghost Jim looking very pleased with himself.

'Tell my Ada I love her to the moon and back,' he says, 'and tell her to look in the custard tin in the larder. I was saving up for a day at the seaside. Tell her to take the kids to Weston, like we planned.'

'Ooh, the sneaky so-and-so,' Ada says, but she's smiling now. Blythe Bumble, however, barrels her way towards us, torpedoing people out of her way like a submarine.

'*Now* we should go,' I say to Lemon, who looks at me, astonished. She drops my hand and as soon as we make it to the exit we run.

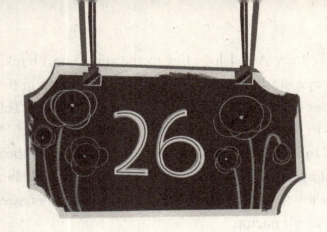

Back at the grotto, the atmosphere between my sister and me is odd and icy. The other girls keep their distance and I half expect to see their footsteps picked out in frost as they tiptoe around us.

'I *had* to come,' I explain, when, for the millionth time, she tells me I shouldn't have. 'We thought you were *dead*. That boy, Wilf –' I pause, remembering another reason to be annoyed – 'who, by the way, you *obviously* know very well, is probably going to get blamed for your disappearance, so what choice did I have? I did it if only to stop him going for the long drop.' I rub at my neck.

'And you say Bessie just . . . *let* you come?' Lemon has changed into flannel breeches and a grey knitted jumper, that stupid, fussy, old-fashioned (annoyingly *cool*) dress folded up on the floor. 'I don't understand. Why would she do that?' Her brow furrows under her new fringe.

'I told you,' I say, keeping my voice light. 'Mam's got a touch of the flu and besides,' I add, airily, 'Bessie obviously knows I'm mature enough to be trusted.'

'Ha!' scoffs Lemon. 'And within five minutes of being here you lose the money she gave you and get yourself a head injury.'

I ignore her and instead point at her dress on the floor. 'Why did you bring that with you? And why, *why* did you do that to yer hair?' I make myself look at it and recoil with a dramatic intake of breath, like I'm forcing myself to look at Badger's poo on a walk. Lemon's hair, her beautiful, swishy river of hair, is gone.

'It was a disguise.'

'You could've just worn a hat,' I say, mumbling into my jumper.

'Ha! I said that,' trills Velvet from the other side of the grotto. 'Sorry!' She circles the air with her finger. 'Sound bounces around here. My apologies.'

Lemon's cheek dimples. 'I suppose I *could* have worn a hat,' she concedes. 'But this felt . . . more exciting.' She strokes at her head like it's a cat. 'I fancied a change, that's all.'

'You absolute hypocrite,' I say. 'You were livid at Mam for cutting 'ers but yours is even shorter!' It's true; Lemon's hair sits just below her earlobe and, where Mam's is one length, Lemon now has a fringe in a straightish line above her eyebrows. I peek at it with one eye closed, like it pains me too much to see with both. It actually looks rather swish and modern, but I'd never tell her that. 'Here,' I say, ferreting in my pocket. 'You can stick some of it back on.' I throw the shorn-off ponytail at her and she catches it, astonished.

'How did you . . .?' She grips her hair in her hand. 'Ohhh . . . I cut it off on Wilf's boat . . . And Wilf brought you to Gloucester.'

'Yes.'

She frowns, annoyed. 'I thought he'd keep his mouth shut.'

'I didn't give him much choice.'

'Even so, I did warn him not to.'

I think back. '*I'm to take you nowhere*, he said. I thought it was a funny thing to say.' I glare at my sister. 'Why? Why did you tell him not to help me when he'd helped you?'

'Because, *Ninny*, I was trying to keep you safe and I thought he understood that.' She glowers at me. 'What did you do? Threaten him with the law?'

I clamp my mouth shut. That's exactly what I did.

'Nin! Poor Wilf. Fine, I'll tell you what happened. I saw the photographs of the girls in the paper . . . yes, I went in Mam's handbag. I told you the mams were hiding something, didn't I? Anyway, then I knew for sure there was a mystery to be solved and . . .' She pauses, a flush creeping up her neck. 'I was *bored*, Nin. Really, really bored.' Her shoulders slump and her head lolls backwards to demonstrate exactly how very bored she was. 'I thought it'd be a day or two of adventure, but then I met up with the girls and realized it was a bigger deal than I'd thought. The Righteous *are* behind the kidnappings, and I chose to stay to help sort it all out.' She shrugs, as if all of this is perfectly normal.

'Why didn't you tell me, instead of running away? I could've helped. I know we argued, but I didn't think you hated me enough to leave me behind.'

Lemon recoils. 'I don't *hate* you, you twit.'

'But when I tried to reach you, you know, with our hide-and-seek rhyme, you shut me out.'

'Of course I did.' She sniffs dismissively, then casually tosses her hair. It swings back and hits her in the eye and I swallow a smirk. 'I didn't tell Jessie about our Devona link in case she thought it was too much of a risk and sent me home. By then I suspected The Righteous might be after *us* and I wanted to keep you safe.'

I've no answer to that.

'You're welcome,' she says with a serene smile. 'As the older twin, it's my duty. The mams would agree, I'm sure.' Her face suddenly drops. It's like her brain has taken a breath and all of the words that came before are crashing into each other. 'Flu?' she says, eyes filled with worry. 'Normal flu, or *Spanish* flu?'

Hearing Lemon say it out loud makes my stomach flip-flop. We lock eyes. Is it *my* pounding heart I can hear or hers? It doesn't take a mystical twin connection for us to realize we are both feeling the same thing. We're terrified.

Maeve is concerned about the bump on my head. She walks her fingers through a shelf of glass jars and bottles, chooses one, lifts its lid to sniff the contents then brings it over. Agnes has been teaching her, she explains. 'This'll bring the bruise out,' she says, scooping a smear of minty-smelling gloop on to her finger and dabbing it on to my forehead. 'Me gran was into herbs and things. Got called a witch.' She wipes her hand on a rag and nods thoughtfully. 'Which she was, but still. Folk can be mean.' I think of how Maeve was written about in the newspaper. *One of them creepers . . . likely up to high jinks.* Yes, folk *can* be mean. The balm tingles on my skin, cooling and hot at the same time.

'They've changed their name,' she says, hitching up her dungarees as she tucks her legs under to sit next to us. 'The Righteous, I mean. Sorry, couldn't help but overhear. Calling themselves the TR Society now, or some nonsense. They have a symbol.' She takes her finger and draws a curly, interwoven T and R into the dust on the stone floor. At first glance it looks like the shape of a cross.

'Wait . . . I've seen that sign somewhere,' I whisper. 'On a plate by the front door belonging to a doctor, I think. He threw vegetable peelings at me —'

'Sounds about right,' mutters Maeve. 'It's always the *respectable* ones.'

And I think too about Detective Simons' signet ring . . . That had a similar symbol, I'm sure of it.

Before bed that evening, I learn that there are several entrance points to the tunnels; 'ins' as the girls call them. Jessie shows me a map of the city, on which they've marked each of the 'ins' with a red circle as they came across them, mapping the tunnels with dotted lines. I trace the routes with a finger, something nagging at the back of my mind, a recognition that I can't quite catch hold of.

In bed – a bunk shared with my sister – I think of the map again, but it's so late that sleep drags me away from any clear thought. I rub at tired eyes with the heel of my hand, whisperling ghosts acting as moving night lights, gently illuminating the grotto.

'I'm scared, Nin,' Lemon whispers suddenly. 'I've been scared since Ivy died. Scared and sad. That's why I came to Gloucester.' She puts her thumb in her mouth and reaches for a lock of hair to twirl, but it's too short. 'I thought if I could fix *something*, I wouldn't be scared no more and I'd go back to being brave and –' her voice catches – 'happy.'

My heart twists like rags on washday. 'I'm so sorry, Lem. I wish you'd spoken to me.' I reach for her hand and she grips it tightly. It feels good to be close to her again.

'Don't tell no one, will you? I've got a reputation to protect.' I smile in the dark, and promise to keep her secret. 'I should have said something. I'm sorry. But you knew I wasn't dead, didn't you?' She reaches under her pillow and brings out her shorn ponytail. She waggles it at me and it tickles my nose. 'You could feel me through *this*, Nin. Something that's no longer on my head. We're twins. *Whisperling* twins. Don't tell me you really thought I was dead.'

She's right, of course. I can feel my sister in my heart, all the time, but for a while panic made me forget that.

'You'd feel it,' she says, casually. 'Like I did.'

'*What?*' I push myself up on my elbows, fully awake now.

'When you had your accident,' she says, voice cracking. 'It was like being ripped in two. I felt you leave me.'

I had no idea. 'You never said.'

'I didn't have to, yer big ninny.' She squeezes my hand and even through my gloves I feel ribbons of energy wrapping themselves round us, locking us together. 'Because then I felt you come back.'

'Together forever?'

'Forever together.'

This time when she sticks her thumb in her mouth I pass her a length of my hair to twirl and we both fall asleep.

# 27

*Trudge, trudge, trudge.*

*Trudge, trudge, trudge.*

*Trudge, trudge, trudge —*

*That noise, that incessant marching noise!*

*Swarming, writhing creatures, churning the water, slippery arms grabbing at me, pulling me towards them, dragging me in, shaking me, shaking me, calling my name, 'Nin, Nin, wake up, Nin, for goodness' sake, you massive flamin' nitwit —*

'Wake UP!'

I come to, eyes bleary and leaden with sleep, heart thumping in my chest. This isn't the first morning I've woken with a start; two days have now gone by. Bessie's deadline has long passed and my nerves are as ragged as the hem on Wilf's trousers. Lemon is shaking my shoulder, nose almost pressed to mine.

'I'm awake, I'm awake! Get off me! Yuck!'

Sticky red marks splatter her clothes – *oh my goodness, are you hurt?* – but no, 'It's paint, you idiot!'

She's been off with Maeve and Flo on something they call the 'red run' – replicating the painted red Cs that The Righteous and their supporters daub on houses to indicate there's a whisperling inside.

'The least we can do is try and slow them down while we figure out what they're up to,' explains Lemon as she steps out of a boiler suit and removes the hat from over her short crop. She swings a paint can, like she's trying to hypnotize me. 'And if *everyone* has a red C on their front door, that'll confuse them, won't it?'

I tell her that must've been what was on the side of our pub, the pink smudge I saw, where the mams had tried to clean it off. They'd marked us too. *They know we're whisperlings.*

'What's the matter, did you get caught?'

'No, not us, we're fine.' She shoves a newspaper at me. 'Look,' she says, jabbing an impatient finger on the page. 'It's Wilf. He's been arrested.'

I sit up and reach for my glasses, hooking the metal arms over my ears.

'I *told* you we should tell the police you're alive!' I mutter furiously. 'This could have *all* been avoided'. It's bad enough we've yet to send word back to the mams, having both decided that we may well be safer here, underground, than back in Oakdean-on-Severn, if we're on the radar of The Righteous. Mam being unwell is a different matter. In the gloomy early hours where dark thoughts lurk, I imagine the reason that Bessie allowed me so freely to come to Gloucester was to find Lemon and bring her home in time to say goodbye to Mam before she dies. A thought I can't share in case it's true, so instead I dampen my pillow with tears, night after night.

'It won't help,' my sister says. 'There's talk that The Righteous have already infiltrated the police and besides, he hasn't been arrested for that.'

'He hasn't?' I look down at the newspaper, but the words jump about on the page. 'What has he done?'

'It's the army that's got him, Nin. He went AWOL – absent without leave.'

'What? What will they do to him? Will he be fined, or made to go back to the war?' The thought of Wilf having to return to the front is too awful to contemplate. He's just a *boy*.

'No.' Lemon shakes her head, tears filling her eyes. 'It's worse than that. If he's found guilty, Nin, he'll be shot for desertion.'

*Shot?*

I'm horrified. 'This is all my fault!' I pull my blanket over my head. 'All my fault! If I hadn't made him, *threatened* him to bring me to Gloucester, this wouldn't have happened.'

'No,' says Lemon, pulling the cover off me. She slumps on the floor. 'It's no one's fault. If he'd told us, maybe we could have done something. Made him go far away instead of helping him hide in the woods and the stables.'

'In the stables?' My mind unlocks a memory of flattened patches of straw. 'That was him? I thought it was Badger.'

Lemon shakes her head. 'No. He'd been in there, on and off, most of the autumn.'

'Why didn't you tell me?'

She shrugs. 'I don't know. It seemed more exciting, it being my secret, that's all. Sorry.'

'Is it bad?' asks Maeve, reading the newspaper article while she cradles a cup of Velvet's nettle tea in her hands. 'Going AWOL?'

'It sure is,' explains Jessie, an authority on all things military, because her father's in the army, she's told me, and holds a senior rank. 'Being absent without leave means he ran away from his fellow soldiers. What a coward.'

Anger boils inside me. 'Take that back.'

'I will not. He signed up to do a job, and it's awful and, yeah, I wish none of them had to do it, but they can't *all* run away.' Her voice cracks. 'Where would that leave the ones who stay and fight? How much harder would it be for them?'

'But what will happen to him?' asks Velvet. 'He won't really be shot, will he?'

'Probably,' says Jessie. 'That's what they do to deserters in the First World War.'

Velvet gasps in horror. 'No! That can't be!' She grabs the newspaper from Maeve, running her finger along the lines of text. 'Ugh. This is barbaric.'

'The report doesn't give his age, Nin,' says Lemon. 'What if they don't know how young he is?'

'What do you mean?' asks Flo. 'And what do *you* mean, Jessie – *First* World War? How many are we going to have?'

'Great War, sorry. Just an American term, I guess.'

'He'd have told them how old he was, surely?' I say, grabbing Lemon by the arm. I remember how quick I was to judge him when I first met him. I thought he may have killed my sister, for goodness' sake. 'But what if they don't believe him?'

'How old is he?' asks Jessie.

'Fourteen. He's fourteen.'

Maeve gives a little shake of her head. 'He can't be, that's rubbish!' she says with a snort. 'How long was he out there for?'

'Eighteen months,' says Lemon. 'He was twelve when he volunteered.'

'*Twelve?*' Jessie shakes her head 'God, no. I've heard of kids signing up, you know, adding a year or two to their their age, but . . .' She trails off. 'My kid brother is twelve.'

'We've got to help him. We *have* to try,' I insist.

'Where's he being held?'

'It says in the paper he's in Gloucester Gaol.' I look up. 'Why there? If it's an army matter, why haven't they taken him back to the barracks?'

Something doesn't add up, but there isn't time to work out what.

## 28

That afternoon, with Flo as our guide (and 'protector', she stated, sharpening a stick with a penknife, which caused me to wonder if there are vampires to watch out for, too), Lemon and I go to Wilf's sister's house. Orla regards us, warily, as well she might; we both wear boy's clothing, our hair tucked away under caps, and it thrills me, and infuriates me, how much safer I feel winding through the narrow, wet alleyways of the city dressed like this.

We explain ourselves. In exchange, Orla, wrestling a fat-legged baby as he dabs tiny feet on her lap like a dancing puppet, tells us about her little brother. How before the war Wilf had split his time between helping his dad on the boat and selling newspapers on the corner of Westgate Street.

'Sometimes, for a change, 'e'd bag a pitch at Shire Hall, where 'e'd lean against a pillar an' pretend to be in ancient Greece. Or that museum in London what's got a fake dinosaur called Dippy.' He'd wondered if he could make his fortune there, or was it the same as here? Where the fancy buildings are a tease an' the hill to climb from poor to rich is too steep, too slippery.

He'd hoped to find his father or at least his fortune in France. When he came back, though, he weren't the same.

'A lot of them are like that,' Orla goes on, 'can't speak, can't stop shakin'. 'E should never've gone. 'E were just a child, but there was no tellin' 'im. Next thing, our Wilf finds 'imself as crew on a hospital boat, an' one day, when it docked in Gloucester, 'e were so surprised to find 'imself back here, his home town, 'e jus' got off the boat an' kept walkin'. When 'e knocked on the door I nearly fell through the floor! Told us 'e were on leave. I remember there was a storm that firs' night an' 'e hid under the table, crying like a baby cos 'e couldn't stand the noise of the howlin' an' the windows rattlin'.

'That's when 'e told me,' she says. 'Confessed 'e'd gone AWOL an' couldn't go back. They'd said 'e had to go back in the trenches an' 'e said 'e couldn't stand it. 'E'd been all right on the boats, but the trenches are like hell on earth. I said to 'im then *Tell them you're a kid an' shouldn't 've been there in the firs' place!* But no, 'e said it were too late, 'e were a soldier now an', besides, they wouldn't care.

'A few days later, 'e told me about another lad who'd legged it sometime after a big battle, dressed 'imself in civilian clothes to try an' pass 'imself off as local. When they found 'im, they dragged 'im back. Paid the ultimate price, 'e did. 'E were sixteen. Shouldn't 've been there at all, like our Wilf. Wilf saw it all. The other lad was his mate, see.'

And on top of all that, while Wilf was away, the family lost Mabel. 'The Spanish flu,' Orla explains, picking up a photograph of a tiny little girl in a white cotton dress embroidered with flowers. 'Doted on her, 'e did, said 'e should never 've left her. That's why 'e nicked your money, Nin. We thought the baby was getting sick an' all. 'E were desperate.' She looks up with glassy eyes. ''E were so sorry about that.' Then she touches Mabel's photo, strokes her little daughter's face with her finger.

'Inseparable, they were,' Orla says, and I nod.

I met Mabel, when Wilf brought me here, although I don't tell Orla this. A little girl in a white cotton dress who here, now, as transparent as morning mist, sits solemnly at her mother's feet and waits for news of her beloved uncle Wilf. The ghost of his niece Mabel.

*Inseparable.*

29

By the time Flo, Lemon and I leave Orla's, night-time is spreading over an already ashen sky, like an ink spill over blotting paper. The weather's taken a turn for the worse; water bounces off the ground like rubber balls, so any bit of me that's covered on its way down is splashed on its way back up.

'Where is she?' says Lemon, squinting.

It's proving a bit tricky to spot our guide. Helping us find our way back from Wilf's sister's house to the grotto is a regal-looking spirit in a sparkly golden crown, who we've decided is a medieval princess, or perhaps one of Henry the Eighth's wives. I slip off a glove and reach for my sister's hand. The effect is immediate; the ghost princess sparkles before us like she's been sprinkled with shimmering fairy dust. 'There she is!' says Lemon, and the princess turns and waves, wafting in front of a shop window, an advertisement for Pears Soap visible through her middle.

It's a genius idea having whisperling ghosts guide new members of the Creeper Gang into the tunnels, and one that makes sense: the spirits can't get caught by The Righteous, but they can be seen by other whisperlings.

'Creeper ghosts can be seen by living creepers, no matter how weak or strong their gift is,' explained Jessie, as I tried hard not to flinch at the use of the reclaimed word. I hadn't realized it, but the bent-necked girl whose ghost I saw in Bull Lane was also a guide. It was she who lured me off the street so that Flo could find me.

We scoot from shop doorway to shop doorway. The streets are glossy with water, street lamps casting yellow reflections like eggs in a pan and, for the life of me, I cannot get a stupid nursery rhyme out of my head:

Doctor Foster went to Gloucester
In a shower of rain;
He stepped in a puddle,

Right up to his middle,
And never went there again.

We weave through the streets of Gloucester and my stomach growls as we pass a chip shop, which Flo says is the famous chippy that drew her to the city. It does indeed smell delicious, and I decide right there to treat everyone – Wilf, his family, creepers and all – to a chippy tea when this is over.

*Wilf.* Lemon and I have written a letter, to be delivered to the barracks, confirming Wilf's true age, and Orla and Reggie, Wilf's sister and her husband, have an urgent appointment to speak to their local MP. We have *got* to help him. If anything happens to him, I'll never forgive myself.

*March, march, march. Trudge, trudge, trudge –*

Not that noise again! I put my hands to my ears and scrunch my eyes shut.

There's a tug at my arm. 'What are you doing, you prat?' I open my eyes to see Flo's face about an inch from mine.

'Is it . . . ghost soldiers?' I whisper, not wanting to look. I haven't the energy for a ghostly battalion.

'No,' says Flo, cobalt-blue eyes peering at me as if she's looking at a particularly stupid new species of prat through a magnifying glass. 'It is actual flesh-and-blood human beings.' She steps to one side. 'See?'

She's right. A procession of people, women mainly, striding purposefully through the city. There *is* something military-like about them, even if they're dressed in civilian clothes. My eyes flick from one row to the next, barely able to keep focus as they stream past. There must be a hundred of them, if not more. 'It's an anti-war protest,' explains Flo, pointing at a placard that reads STOP THE WAR in bold letters. 'There've been several over the last few weeks. These people are really brave. The government don't like it at all.' Flo ineffectually stands on her tiptoes to see over the crowd. 'We need to get out of here – it isn't safe for us,' she says.

'Oh, come on,' says Lemon, tugging at my sleeve, eyes shining with excitement. She walks backwards towards the crowd, pulling me with her. 'Where's the harm?'

'No,' says Flo, 'we really shouldn't. The police –' But the rest of her sentence is swallowed by the horse-like clomping of a thousand hobnail boots on cobbles.

It's hard not to be swept along.

'Join us!' invites a woman. She's carrying a placard that says MOTHERS FOR PEACE, and we shrug helplessly at Flo and fall in line. She has three sons at the front, the woman tells us, and, above shouts of 'Bring our boys home!' and 'No more cannon fodder!', we tell her about Wilf. When she's listened to our story, she vows to do what she can. 'We have to be a voice for the voiceless,' she says, and Flo, Lemon and I exchange a glance. *A voice for the voiceless* . . . I suppose that's what whisperlings are. I feel a tiny rush of pride.

'We're going to the Guildhall,' our new friend tells us. 'It's where Gloucester council meets. We've tipped the newspapers off too. Let them try and ignore us *now*!' and she shakes her head defiantly.

'Look,' says Flo, craning her neck. 'Over there. Look at those signs!' Without the street lamps it would be too dark to see much, but Lemon reads them out, squinting: ' "Where Are Our Children?" . . . "Find the Missing Girls!" . . . "Whisperlings Are People Too".'

The three of us look at one another, thrilled and scared at the same time. 'They're for *us*, Nin, for the girls!' Lemon cries. I wish we had a placard to hold; it feels good to march, shoulder to shoulder.

'What's that about?' I ask, pointing to another placard in the crowd. Bury Our Boys. Then I notice other, similar slogans, too: Respect the Fallen . . . Bring the Bodies Home.

Our friend explains that the army is no longer allowed to return the bodies of fallen soldiers for burial at home. Instead, war graves are dug for them in France or Belgium. 'They can't come home,' I whisper. 'Those poor boys. Their poor families.' I'm about to ask Lemon if she thinks that may be why quite so many ghosts of soldiers have been coming to our messagings when –

*Peep! Peeeeeep!*

Police.

The crowd surges forward and for a horrible moment it feels like I'm being swept along by a powerful current of water, and, stupidly, I hold my breath in case I'm pulled under. Panic rattles in my chest.

'I bleedin' said being here was dangerous for us, didn't I?' snaps Flo, sounding angry and scared at the same time. She positions herself between Lemon and me like a linchpin, hooking each of us by the arm, and weaves us through the protesters, aiming to get back to the pavement. There's a push and a shove and I'm untethered, lifted from my feet and carried off to one side.

'Nin!' shouts Lemon. Flo reaches for me but I'm bobbling through bodies like a cork on the ocean. The crowd pushes forward until I can only just see the top of her cap and by the time I scrabble my way out of the crowds, Flo and Lemon are nowhere to be seen.

I'm entirely, completely lost.

I look upward, seeking the outline of the cathedral to give me some sense of direction, but the sky is battleship grey and the moon and stars are smothered by charcoal storm clouds. The crowd thins as the march continues to the Guildhall and soon the street is empty. I blink, hard. It's getting darker. The glow from the gas lamps is fading; did the storm blow them out? I look up at the closest lamp, listening for the hiss of doused flame, but hear nothing but the hammer of rain against cobble, glass and metal. I blink again.

Something black and raggedy is crawling over the lamps, snuffing them out one by one. The skin on my neck prickles. It's coming towards me. I walk backwards, not daring to take my eyes from it, although all I want to do is turn and run.

Water seeps through the eyelets in my boots, soaking my stockings. I glance down; the deep puddle I stand in is black and oil-like. There is movement in it. I blink, wiping my glasses with the back of my hand as something in the water shimmers and shifts. Are those . . . *lights* in the water? Like teeny, twinkling fallen stars? I quickly check behind me; is something throwing its reflection into the water? But there's nothing there, and it's a cloudy, starless night. I look back up to the ragged creature stalking me. It's drawn closer since the last glance, like an evil game of grandmother's footsteps, but I can't resist another look at what is happening under my feet. As I look more closely, faces swirl in the puddle, their mouths open and yawning in an endless, silent scream. But it isn't a scream. And it isn't silent. I squint, certain I'm imagining it, but I'm not. Like the strange, drowning ghosts from the docks, they're saying one word, over and over and over.

'*Run!*'

It snaps at my heels, this thing, snuffing out the light so quickly I can barely make it to the next lamp before I'm plunged into darkness again and again and again. My heart thumps in my chest. What the heck *is* it? Like a bewildered fawn, I skitter through the city until my legs are so tired and wobbly I've no choice but to stop for a minute. I check behind me with one eye shut, needing to know where it is but not *really* wanting to see it . . . I *can't* see it. I look left and right, up and down, even under my feet and through both eyes this time. It's gone. The creature has gone. At least, for now.

Relief flows over me like I've stepped into a warm bath and I lean against the wall next to me. The wall belongs to an industrial-looking building set back from the road. It has enough of an overhang to provide a bit of shelter as I wipe the rain from my glasses and rub my freezing hands together. They're so cold they prickle. But the rubbing doesn't help, and so I blow on them – and it's like blowing on the embers of a fire. The prickling feeling travels up my arms, over my shoulders, down my back, up into my neck, through my scalp. It's like I've rolled in snow and then jumped into a hot bath.

Something is *very* wrong.

I slip off a glove and press my hand against the neat red bricks. My heart tugs, a bit like when I feel the invisible thread between Lemon and me.

And there's a noise: *tap, tap, tap*. I press my ear to the wall. *Tap, tap, tap*. Then I realize: I didn't stop running; I *was* stopped. The creature chased me here. It as good as snapped at my heels like a sheepdog herding a runaway lamb. But why? I step back, and look up at the building. It looks well kept and featureless. What – or who – is in there?

And then, before I know it, I'm knocking.

The door opens.

'I knew it was you!' The mysterious glowing girl holds out her hands. She looks like a burnished angel. 'I felt you getting closer to me,' she says, smiling. 'Did you feel me, too?'

I nod, dumbly.

'We're going to be great pals, I know it! I'm Charlotte. Charlotte Crawley. But you can call me Lottie.'

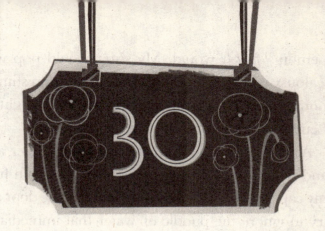

I'm sure Flo was wrong about Lottie. She isn't a 'wrong 'un' or 'bad news'; she's unusual and fascinating and, *surely*, one of us? I feel a stab of annoyance at my new Creeper Gang friends. For those who know what it's like to be bullied, perhaps they've been too quick to judge this girl.

Lottie's dark blue dress is a whisper away from threadbare, slightly off the shoulder and fitted to the hip, from where it flares into a wide fishtail that swishes against the floorboards as she walks. I'm very aware of my boyish clothes, although Lottie hasn't remarked on them. She looks very grown up. In spite of her poise, she's only a few years older than me, sixteen at the most. Maybe *she's* got a dressing-up box, too. The mams would not approve;

Lemon *definitely* would. My sister would pop with jealousy if she knew I had a friend as interesting as Lottie, and as I'm ushered inside the thought of Lemon's narked face warms my innards.

A maid tucks her feather duster under her arm and politely bobs a welcome. I shake the rain from my cape, hang it on a coat stand next to the door and try to ignore the puddle of water that immediately pools underneath it. I smile apologetically at the maid as we pass her and she shrugs, unbothered.

*Tap, tap, tap.*

I scrub at my ears. 'What's that noi–'

'Like it?' interrupts Lottie, spreading her arms theatrically as if introducing the building as a person. It's a beautiful, wonky old place, far more impressive on the inside than the outside. The way the timber beams criss-cross the white walls reminds me of the lattice on a Bakewell tart. A galleried landing splits the room in two, and way, way above it is a cathedral-like ceiling laced with wooden struts and cross-beams. The effect is dizzying. It's like being in a galleon on the high seas. I pull my eyes away; if I look any longer I'll be seasick.

I follow Lottie over the uneven floor. There's a crunch underfoot and as I lift my boot to look something sparkles in the floorboard. 'It was a pin factory, back in the day,' Lottie tells me. 'Sometimes the past leaves behind a memory or two,' she says, meaningfully. I half expect her to pull out a handkerchief and dab at her eyes.

*Tap, tap, tap.*

'Can you hear that?' I ask. Lottie shrugs and says something about the rain. I shiver and try not to look too closely into the shadowy corners. She may be a bit dramatic, but she isn't wrong about this place holding memories.

'What's in there?' I ask, moving to turn the handle of a door that's almost concealed in the panelling.

'Oh no,' she snaps, gripping my arm, 'we can't go into the basement.'

I flinch back at her sharp tone.

'I'm so sorry,' she says, softening. 'I didn't mean to snip.' She tilts her head and puts her free hand to her tummy as if in discomfort from her corset. 'Small spaces remind me of my mother, that's all.' She sighs wistfully and releases her grip on my arm. 'She's passed on, you see.'

I offer my condolences as she steers me away from the basement door. 'Afflicted with the claustrophobia, she was, thanks to a . . . situation where she was locked in the bog ... er, water closet for hours.' She grumbles under her breath. 'Daft old bat. Thank God I'm nothing like her.'

Lottie shows me through to a small sitting room, where a side table is covered with a white tablecloth and laid for tea. A swirl of golden biscuits is spread on a plate, like a hand of playing cards. Was she expecting me?

She gestures for me to sit next to her. 'Milk, sugar?' She pours tea through a little silver strainer and the gleam of her face is reflected in the silver lustre of the teapot. It's all over her, the whisperling glow. I've never seen anything like it. It reminds me a bit of a spirit on its burn, but Lottie is very much alive and so neither a new ghost nor one that's returned, for good reasons or mischief.

I take a sip of my tea. It's extremely sweet and oddly perfumed. I take another glug, and another. It's weird, but moreish.

*Tap, tap, tap.*

What *is* that? I swish a hand round my head as if batting off a fly. Lottie stares at me so hard it's a bit annoying, but I don't say anything. She might take away this delicious tea and that would be terrible. Besides, her skin is so pretty and her dress so *cool* that I don't want to upset her. It would be fun to have a friend that is just mine. Lemon had Ivy, after all. Come to think of it, Lemon had Wilf first, too. *And* the Creeper Gang . . . That decides it. Lottie is *my* friend. I drum my fingers on the arm of the chair. What do new friends talk about . . . ?

'So, do you like being a creep—'

Lottie's left eye flickers, like a tiny fly has landed on it.

I grapple for the correct word. '. . . A whisper – thingy?'

'Well, yes, it's such a privilege, wouldn't you say?' she replies through a rather stiff smile. I can't remember if she knows I'm a creeper or if it's even something I should be telling anyone. It's like a door in my brain has opened and bits of it are falling out. I put a hand to my ear, in case that's where the exit is.

'Oh!' She claps her hands together. 'I have something for you! I almost forgot.' She takes a chain from round her neck. There's a little key hanging from it, and she uses this to unlock a small bureau. From a narrow drawer, she removes a dinky velvet pouch, which she places in front of me. 'Open it. It's yours.'

I loosen the cord and tip out what's inside. It's a necklace: a crystal, purplish in colour, threaded on to a silver chain. I pool the chain in my gloved hand; it's pretty, but I don't understand. 'It isn't me birthday,' I say and Lottie tinkles with laughter.

'I know, silly. Although, wouldn't that have been a funny coincidence? I wanted to give you a symbol of our friendship.' She dips a hand inside the top of her dress and pulls out a matching necklace. 'See? We're the same, you and I.' She takes the necklace from my open hand.

'We are?'

'Of course! I mean, look at me!' She sits back down and points to her face. 'You can see my glow, can't you?'

I squint, and her face swims in front of me like she's melting. 'You are the very glowiest of all the glowing things that have ever glowed,' I tell her solemnly. I burp, cover my mouth and blow the foul-tasting belch to the side. Lottie puts a hand to her nose.

'And it isn't easy, finding other whisperlings to talk to.' She looks at me from underneath her eyelashes. 'Have, uh, *you* spoken to any other whisperlings while you've been in town?'

I squeeze my lips together between my finger and thumb and shake my head. It's not a lie. The girls are creepers, not whisperlings, and I'm not to tell anyone about them or their hiding place. Not even Lottie. The deceit makes my armpits prickle.

'Can I tell you a secret?' Lottie leans over and fastens my new necklace round my neck. 'Now that we're friends.'

I nod, trying not to move too much. My tummy feels like it's being stirred with a big spoon.

'I'm a whisperling, first and foremost,' she says. 'But I'm also a businesswoman. An *entrepreneur*. I'm looking to the future. I would like to find another whisperling as skilful as myself.' She pauses, the light from a paraffin lamp bouncing off her skin, making it sparkle. 'And open an *on-demand* spirit communication portal.'

A bubble of laughter gurgles in my belly. Everything is suddenly very funny! I drain my cup; she pours me another, and offers me a biscuit. I take a bite, and it's the best shortbread I have ever tasted! She's so generous. I *must* tell the Creeper Gang about this place. Oh! We could have a party! A creeper party. A 'creeparty'. I stifle my giggles.

*Tap, tap, tap.*

I stick my fingers in my ears. 'La, la, la!'

'Everything all right, lovely?' She looks at me earnestly, like Badger when he wants a nibble of something. Maybe that's what she wants! I'm so rude, eating all the shortbread. I break a bit off and pop it into her mouth. 'Good girl,' I say.

'Thank you.' Lottie draws a lace-edged handkerchief from her sleeve, coughs and turns her head to dab at her mouth. 'Do excuse me.' She takes a sip from her cup, stands up and walks towards a jungle of houseplants in the corner of the room. After swilling the liquid round her mouth she spits it out into the pot of an unsuspecting aspidistra. 'Stuck in my tooth,' she explains, coming back and laying the frilly white square on the table. 'Now, where were we?'

*You were telling me your stupid idea*, I say in my head but I can't make my voice work. Instead, I take a big sip of tea and give her a thumbs up and she claps her hands together, delighted. 'I knew you and I would get along. You're a visionary, like me,' she says. 'Imagine it – a centre – here, probably – where people can visit, sit in a little booth and have a whisperling contact whichever ghost they like.'

'Don't be daft,' I say with a nasty-tasting hiccup. At least, that's what I *try* to say. What comes out is something like 'Dohnbydaff'. I scrub at my tongue with the back of my hand. 'Dohn-wuk-like-tha.' *Whisperlings aren't telephone exchanges.* I giggle, expecting Lottie to join in, but she doesn't.

'Oh?' says Lottie, coolly. 'And how *does* it work?'

I suddenly feel *very* warm. I breathe in through my nose, then out through my mouth, slowly. 'Why y'askin' me?' I manage. Being a whisperling, she should know you can't *demand* any spirit should talk to you. She should *also* know that whisperlings aren't told the finer details of the afterlife. *No one* should have that sort of knowledge.

I squint at Lottie. As well as the strange, shimmering glow of her skin there's also a dull smudge round her temples, easily mistaken for a smut of soot or hair pomade. She leans towards me, studying my face like there's something written there. 'I'm asking because I know that there are *some* whisperlings who *can* do just that. Isn't that right, Miss Esmond?'

The floor rushes up to meet me and I put my teacup down with a clatter. I know what Lemon and I can do is special – we do draw spirits to us, somehow, even those long from their burn and far from home – but we can't *make* them come to us. It isn't possible.

'How about we play a little game?' suggests Lottie.

I can't even speak, so how am I supposed to play a game?

'A special whisperling game.' She pings the pendant round my neck with a fingernail. I feel like a frog in the company of a very hungry snake. 'Wait there just a moment.' She claps her hands in delight. 'Ooh, I'm so excited!'

'Water, please?' A bitter bubble of sick catapults up and down my gullet. I swallow, hard.

'Just have some more tea!'

I shake my head. I can see bits at the bottom of the cup and they taste funny and – oh no . . .

The room whizzes in and out of focus and on leaden legs I barge past Lottie. A second later I'm retching into the rubber plant. In that moment, as my stomach turns inside out, I realize two things.

One: that was *not* normal tea.

And two: I've never told Lottie my name . . . so how on earth does she know it?

*I have to get out of here!*

'I don't feel . . . well . . . at all,' I say slowly, although thanks to the vomiting my head and speech are clearer. 'P'haps . . . I can come back another time, and . . . we can –'

'No,' snaps Lottie. 'It has to be now.' She quickly clears the table of cups and saucers, balancing them on a silver tray which she moves to the top of the bureau.

'I don't *want* to play.' I blink hard, my vision clearing. What was in that tea? My tummy still feels horribly swirly. 'I want to go –' I stop myself. 'Home. I have to go home.'

'And where is home?' she asks, casually.

'Bristol,' I lie, allowing myself a hiccup. 'Near the . . . zoo. And the bridge. I need to catch a train.'

'I know you're lying.' Lottie's expression shifts from day to night. 'My ma used to work in *Bris*tol,' she says, spitting out the word like it burns her tongue. 'Scratching a living for an utter fopdoodle of a man. I vowed never to live like that. Turned me into the woman I am today – independent, powerful . . .' She gazes into the middle distance. 'Anyway, where were we?'

Her hatred of Bristol seemingly forgotten, she steps to the bureau once more. There's that feeling again, like I'm being sucked into a whirlpool. It might be the after-effects of the weird tea, but I don't think so. Lottie opens another drawer and brings something out, a large, rectangular-shaped item wrapped in a black cloth, and the feeling *grows*. She puts it on the table. 'You'll have to take those off,' she says, nodding at my gloves.

I shake my head. From my stomach to my throat is scorched with acid, but my head is finally clear. 'No. Definitely not.'

She pauses, cricking her neck as if about to enter a boxing ring. 'Fine. It's up to you. Now, let's see what you've got –'

There are footsteps in the hallway and into the room walk two men. One could easily be the man who threw the horrible carroty water at me earlier this week. And the other . . .

'Detective Simons!' I say in shock. He doesn't even pretend to look surprised.

'Miss Esmond.' He nods a greeting. 'How nice of you to finally join us.'

*Which Esmond sister do you think I am?* I wonder. Detective Simons knows Lemon is missing – or run away – but does he know that I followed her here, to Gloucester? I called him by his name, so he *should* realize he's met me before at the pub and that I can't therefore be Lemon . . . but then again, he is an idiot. I stare at Lottie, trying to read her mind.

Which Esmond sister does *she* think I am?

'You said you were going to wait until I'd done this bit,' snaps Lottie, bristling. 'This is *my* area of expertise.'

Detective Simons turns the signet ring on his finger. 'Yes, Charlotte, pet, but we need to speed things up, and you do drone on a bit.' The two men nudge each other in the ribs, chuckling.

'Typical woman, what?' laughs the older, hairier man. 'Come along, Lottie, old gal. Time is of the essence.' He peers at me. 'Did you give her too much tonic? She looks a bit green around the gills.'

Lottie flushes. '*No*,' she says defensively. 'She's completely fine.'

'You're only supposed to make 'em docile, not knock 'em out.'

*Docile?* 'What's going on?' I ask, blood thumping in my ears. 'Who *are* you?'

'I, little girl,' says Detective Simons, 'am the head –'

'*Joint* head,' interjects the other man. 'Come along now, Simons, I thought we'd settled that.'

'Apologies, Dr Wibley. *We* –' Simons flashes the other man a pointed glance – 'are the joint heads of the Gloucester and South-West Chapter of the TR Society.'

'The TR Society?'

'You might know us as –' He pauses and takes a breath.

'The Righteous,' interrupts Dr Wibley.

Detective Simons deflates like a child who's had his toy taken away. '*I* was going to say it.' For one moment I expect him to stamp his foot. And *these* are the men that we whisperlings are supposed to fear?

'Shouldn't it be The "R Society"?' I ask, emboldened.

'What?' says Dr Wibley.

'The "R Society". Otherwise you're saying "the" twice, as in "the The Righteous Society".'

'I did tell them that,' says Lottie under her breath.

'Hmm. You really do think yourself something, don't you?' sneers Detective Simons. 'You and the other creeper freaks. We're giving you an opportunity here to prove yourself useful. Great idea little Lottie's got, this *on-demand* spirit thingummy. A real money-spinner. And if you've got enough –' he waggles his fingers – 'of a gift for *that*, then chances are you'll also be able to help us with *our* little project.' He nudges his accomplice. 'Isn't that right, Wibley?'

The older man nods. 'Absolutely. A deal that benefits both parties. And –' he looks to Simons, who nods, as if giving him the go-ahead to say more – 'you wouldn't want to get into trouble now, would you? Or for anything bad to happen to those *mams* of yours.'

'Or to that mangy old dog,' says Simons with a sneer.

I gasp, horrified. Did Simons really just threaten *Badger*? Blood thuds in my ears. I swallow, hard. What chance do I have against them? They may just be two men – and not demons or ghouls – but they are horrible nonetheless, horrible and spiteful and in positions of power.

I chew at my lip so hard that I taste dots of blood. *What can I do?* I glance round, willing a chance of escape to offer itself up – or a weapon to appear, at least, so I can channel my inner Flo – but there's three of them and one of me and thanks to the tea I'm still not feeling my best.

I clear my throat. 'And if I can't do it – whatever it is you want from me – what then?'

Simons shrugs. 'We'll dispose of you like we've done with the others.'

'And we'll keep trying,' adds Wibley, looking at Simons with an earnest, hopeful expression. 'I know we're running out of time, but we can't stop now, can we, Simons?'

'*Dispose*' of me? '*The others*'? Tiny, icy footsteps tiptoe up my spine. As awful as this is, could it be a chance to find out what's happened to the missing girls?

'I'll do it,' I say. 'But just us . . . her and me.' I glare at Lottie. She's a whisperling too, so how *could* she do this to us? 'It won't work if you two men are watching.'

'Excellent,' says Simons, clapping his hands. He guides Dr Wibley to the door. 'Come, sir. There's a bottle of port open in the kitchen. Shall we?'

When the men have gone, I turn to Lottie. 'This is kidnap,' I growl.

'Be quiet!' says Lottie. 'They'll do it, you know. Hurt your mams. And your sister. And –' she swallows – 'your dog.'

Then she lifts a corner of the black cloth covering whatever it was she fetched from the bureau and throws it back. My fingers begin to tingle and scratch, in the same way they did outside the building.

*Tap, tap, tap.* It's getting closer.

*Tap, tap, tap.* Louder.

*Tap, tap, tap.* Insistent.

'Wait,' I say. 'What *is* this?' I raise my smudged glasses to my forehead so I can get a better look. My heart thuds in my ears.

'Oh! So it was *you*!' I say, accusingly. 'You who stole it?' I gaze over its surface, follow the faint impression of the eye and flame. *This* is what I could feel on the other side of the walls, the drag of energy drawing me to it, telling me it was here.

Lottie Crawley and these terrible, awful men somehow have in their possession the Book of Devona.

I'm not afraid, not any more.

This book is filled with the stories and energy of my ancestors and can surely do me no harm. I glare at Lottie and push my hands defiantly on to the swollen leather cover. Even through my gloves, I feel it.

*Tap, tap, tap.*

**Tap, tap, TAP.**

A rumble of energy vibrates and builds, dragging through the air inside the room like a plough furrowing a field. With a shudder, shadows peel and step from the walls, silhouettes of death reanimated. They wisp and gather and . . . Wait! . . . *Look how small they are –*

'Children,' I whisper. 'They're just children.'

I'd sensed something about this place from the moment I stepped through the door: a movement here, a giggle there. A cry. Lottie looks all around, but not at the ghosts. Her face is impassive. Can't she see them? Can't she *feel* this? The air in the room continues to shift and my breath catches in my throat as there's a *clack!* and *boom!* It's in front of me, the whole scene: cross-legged, raggedy children hunched under clattering, whirring contraptions that are halfway between hand-cranked sewing machines and steam engines, the young workers all *tap, tap, tapping* tiny little pin-heads over and over and over again.

A shriek splits the air as something tears past me, something black yet semi-transparent, like the stretched skin of a bat's wing. It's that thing that chased me here, I'm sure of it. The children shrink back from it, like the ghoul is a rock thrown into a pool of minnows, and the industrious scene dissolves away. The creature screeches and swoops, finally perching on Lottie's shoulders like a macabre parrot. She glances up at it and her shoulder drops, although there can be no real weight to it.

'Bloody *hell*!' I say. 'What is *that*?'

She looks at me, triumphant, and slaps my hands away from the book. I make a grab for it but one shove from Lottie and I'm knocked back into my seat, still weakened by the poisonous tea.

'Mr Simons! Dr Wibley!' she trills.

'Yes?' say the men, crowding back into the room.

'Did it work?' asks Wibley, eyebrows raised. He turns his hat in his hands, as if steering a car.

'Of course it didn't,' says Simons, indignantly. 'It never does.' He turns on his heel and makes for the door again. 'I should've known better than to team up with amateurs. I'm off.'

'Wait, Mr Simons,' says Lottie, standing up. She wrings her hands, smiling nervously. 'We've done everything you asked. After all the disappointments and the girls you said weren't quite right . . . well . . .' She nods in my direction. 'We got one.'

Simons pauses, still facing the door. He rocks back on his heel and turns slowly round to face us. Lottie continues. 'She can definitely see him.' She points a finger at the ghoul on her shoulder. 'And her touching that book caused *something* to happen, like he said it would. I *told* you she was one of them special ones. I don't know why you were so reluctant to –'

'Are you questioning my methods, Miss Crawley?' Simons' tone is icy.

'Of course not.' Lottie shakes her head, pink splodges blooming on her cheeks. 'Anyway, she said something about seeing children. In here, in this building. She's the one.'

Wibley claps his hands in delight. He holds his palms to his cheeks, like a child overwhelmed on Christmas morning. 'Finally! After all that searching!' He pushes Simons' shoulder playfully. 'You were a doubting Thomas there for a while, weren't you, Simons? But, look – it's going to happen, at last. We have a top-drawer whisperling and, within days, we'll have The Sight! Isn't it wonderful?'

'Uh, wonderful, yes.' Simons' expression is unreadable. 'There's much to prepare, but yes, soon, definitely soon.' He claps the other man's shoulder with such force that Wibley stumbles forward.

Straightening himself up again, Wibley says, 'Tomorrow, Simons.' Then his tone hardens. 'Everyone is ready, you know that. They've been waiting a long time for this.'

Simons pauses, then nods stiffly in agreement. 'Best get on with the arrangements,' he says. 'I'll see myself out.'

I can't believe it. The book crackles at me, almost with excitement, like a pet reunited with its owner. I'd known the book was important – Mam told us that much. But she'd also told us about its magic, that it has the power to heighten whatever whisperling abilities you already have. That it can even 'unlock the door to the other side', whatever that means. Of course, Lemon and I thought she was talking a load of old tripe.

But not any more.

Dr Wibley stands abandoned in the doorway. 'Right, Wibley old boy,' he says to himself. 'A celebratory drink I think.' He tips his hat in goodbye as if we're friendly acquaintances. The door shuts behind him with a bang.

'Well, they seem nice,' I say sarcastically. 'Exactly the sort of people I'd want to hang about with.'

'Shut up.' Lottie re-wraps the book in its black cover. Her hands are shaking.

'Oh, for heaven's sake, Lottie! Those are bad people! If you *really* think they're going to help you with your ridiculous business plan, you need your head read. They're using you. They've just told you they'll help so you'll help *them*.'

'You don't know what you're talking about. Detective Simons looked out for me when I was at my lowest point. I trust him.'

'Your "lowest point" – after you nicked the book and treacherously told him about its powers, you mean?'

She looks at me, affronted. 'No. I didn't even know Detective Simons back then.' She sucks in her cheeks. 'And it weren't really stealing. I took it to keep it safe, until it was time.' She narrows her eyes at me. 'Which is more than *you* did. Weren't even locked away, never nicked anything so easily in my life.'

I flush at our slapdash security. 'How did you even know about the book?'

Lottie's eyebrow twitches. 'My spirit guide told me.'

'*Spirit guide?* What, that thing on your shoulder?' I hoot with hollow laughter and try to ignore the disgusting thought that the creature knows anything about me.

'Shut your face,' snaps Lottie. 'He's looked out for me more than anyone. Him and Detective Simons. That's what friends do.'

'"*Friends*"? Oh Lottie, have you lost your mind? I don't know what that *thing's* motivation is, but it's nothing good. And as for Simons . . . he's having you help him to kidnap girls. Maybe worse.'

'No. He was just trying to scare you, that's all! The whisperling girls who weren't suitable for the programme were all sent home.'

'There are people out there looking for their children, Lottie. There are reports of missing girls in all the newspapers.' I laugh again, astonished at her naivety. 'They weren't sent *home*. What, do you think Simons and Wibley would let them go free after they've seen whatever it is you're doing here? There are dozens of girls *still* missing.' I pause. 'They'll blame you, you know. Those two. When they get found out.'

'Don't be ridiculous. Half the police are members of the TR Society, and lawyers and judges, too. We look out for each other.'

'"*Each other*"!' I scoff. 'You're a whisperling, Lottie! The Righteous hate our kind.'

She ignores me, and picks up the book to return it to the bureau. I can't let her lock the book away. I make a show of trying to stand, and then fall into a swoon back on to my chair.

'Oh, for heaven's sake,' she says. 'Sit up.'

I cough, tapping my throat. 'Something's stuck,'

I say, wheezing. 'From the tea.' I launch into some full-throated hacking, doubled over like one of the old boys at the pub at their first drag on their cigarette. 'Water – water – water!' *Cough, cough, cough.* 'Please?' I pretend-cough so much that I'm soon coughing for real, heaving as I bring up a gob of rancid-tasting bile. I pull a face, eyes streaming, holding it in my mouth before spitting it into my hand. 'Water!' I plead, genuinely this time.

Lottie passes me a tissue, grimacing like she's caught me pooing on her bed. 'Very well,' she says as I clean myself up. 'I'll get you some. But don't try any funny business. There's no way out.'

As soon as she's out of the room I'm on my feet, scooping the book up with me. I make for the front door, rattle the handle – but it won't open; the men must have the key. I grab my cape from the stand and spin round, not knowing which way to go, and then the maid appears in the hallway, puts a finger to her lips and points her feather duster towards the wall. For a moment I'm confused, but then I see it: the door to the basement, hidden in the panelling. 'Thank you,' I mouth, tiptoeing towards it. I open it as quietly as I can, step through and shut it behind me with a quiet *click*.

It's a basement room, small and brick-lined, scattered with broken chairs, packing cases and bottles grainy with mulched sediment. I grab one of the chairs and push it up against the door, jamming the handle.

The room is utterly unremarkable save a shape picked out in red paint on the floor.

A star.

A five-pointed star.

Witchcraft.

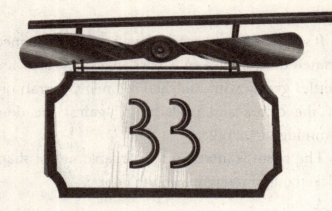

## 33

I scan the basement, trying to locate an exit, but apart from the way I came in there are no obvious ways out. The only thing close to another door is the cast-iron cover of an old bread oven set back in a recess in the opposite wall. I peer round the room again, but my eyes keep tracking back to the bread-oven door. For such a tiny thing, its hinges are huge and the handle curled and ornate, like the door to a toy castle. I place the book carefully on the floor, kneel down beside it and, this time, I slip off my gloves and put them in my pocket. I press my hands to the book's cover.

'Help me,' I whisper. 'Please.'

Energy rushes into my chest. The air in the room shifts and expands but it doesn't feel the same as it did upstairs. Down here, there is only kindness.

A wispy form swims in front of me, like a rolling fog hanging over fields on a chilly morning. Giggling sprinkles the air and one, two, three small shapes step forward from the mist, children, two boys, one girl, as clear as a reflection in the stillest pond. I reach out to the child closest, the girl, and my hand goes through her easily, but not without a slight resistance, as if brushing through cobwebs. 'You shouldn't always be so scared, lady,' she says. The small hatch in the bread oven is entirely visible through her. She tips her head as if to say *In you go*.

'In there? Are you sure?' I try the handle; it won't budge. I try it again; it still won't.

'Once more for luck,' she says with a wink.

I rest my hand on the handle, close my eyes and, with a quiet *click*, it opens.

It's no bigger than a crawl space. But at least it's a *safe* crawl space – a space at the back of a fake bread oven, in the basement of a haunted pin factory, in the middle of Gloucester, where a whisperling traitor works on behalf of a sinister, whisperling-hating bunch of bullies.

As I lie there panicking, the door shuts with a heavier *clunk* and the last sliver of light is snuffed out. *Oh no! The book!* I've left it on the basement floor. I curse my stupidity, but in truth I may not have been able to fit it in here with me. The only way I can move is by digging my toes into the tunnel wall and pushing, worming forward inch by painful inch. When I climbed in, I should've put my hands in front of me like I was going headfirst down a slide, but I didn't, and now my arms are jammed. Added to which I can't see and . . . I'm stuck. Trapped, like a sweep up a chimney.

I'm in total darkness, I can't breathe, *I can't breathe* – No! Come *on*, Nin, you *can* do this. You *have* to!

I blow out slowly as if deflating myself and squash up sideways to try and release an arm. Yes! Success! I do the same on the other side. With both arms free I feel around. There's a wall a fingertip stretch in front of me . . . and a gap to my left . . . *fzzzz . . . What's that noise?* I feel the ground directly in front of me. It falls away, but I can't tell if it's a slope or a drop. *What shall I do?* I can't go back. I can't manoeuvre enough to get through the gap on my left . . . I have no choice. I squeeze my eyes shut and dig and push and dig and . . . oh no . . . I'm falling forward!

*Oof!*

There is nothing. Just the dark.

It's pitch black down here. There are no lights or markings and it's damp. I put a hand to the floor. It's more than damp; it's wet. I listen out, straining my ears. Is that the trickle of an underground spring? What if it's water, with the pressure building like behind a seam down a mine, ready to burst and flood the space I'm in? Panic flutters in my chest. Is this what it was like for Wilf in the trenches? *I'm going to die under here and how is anyone going to find me?* Or, worse, what if Lottie realizes which way I've gone and sends one of her goons after me?

I scootch myself up to a sitting position. I have to move. There's more room here, at least; I can almost stand up. I should leave a marker, just in case. The only things I have with me are my gloves. It feels like leaving part of me behind, but what choice do I have? I tuck one in a gap in the wall. Maybe it's time, anyway.

I slop through the water, head and shoulders scrunched forward, one hand on the wall to follow the lines of the tunnel and the other above my head so I don't hit it on the low ceiling. The water is no higher than my ankles. It's not too bad. It's safe. Perfectly safe. I ignore the panic pounding at my ribs like beaters on a xylophone. Every so often there's a gap in the wall, an offshoot, but I ignore these, deciding that following the main tunnel is the only sensible thing to do.

It feels like I've been walking for hours. I must be making progress. My hand brushes against something soft and I swallow a squeal. I scrunch it in my hand. It's my glove. I shove it angrily into my pocket. I'm back exactly where I started.

And then I hear her. It's like she's knocking on a door in my head.

'Ogethertay oreverfay, oreverfay ogethertay! Ogethertay oreverfay, oreverfay ogethertay!'

Lemon.

I repeat it back to her, over and over and over, keeping my sister's face in my mind the whole time. Our silly pig Latin hide-and-seek chant.

'Ogethertay oreverfay. Oreverfay ogethertay.'

'Together forever. Forever together.'

My sister is looking for me.

All I have to do is wait.

34

'Nin? Nin? That you?' Light from a miner's helmet flares in my face. 'It's her! I told you, I told you!' Lemon is ecstatic. She kneels in front of me and squeezes me into a tight hug. I shut my eyes, dazzled. 'Together forever,' she whispers. 'Ogethertay oreverfay.'

'Forever together,' I reply. 'Oreverfay ogethertay.'

'Come on, help me get her up.' Velvet crouches next to my sister. 'I can't believe it worked,' she says, peering at me like I'm a curiosity in a cabinet.

'It's a twin thing,' I say, woozily.

'Twin thing or not –' Velvet puts a hand under my chin to tip my face up to the light – 'if you keep this up you're going to be more bump than forehead.'

I half walk and half allow myself to be dragged back to the grotto through an impossible-to-remember twist of tunnels.

When we get back, Jessie's orders are sharp.

'Flo, get up there, use the shepherd's hook to make sure that cover is good and closed, and backfill as close to the entry point as you can. A bucket of bricks and gravel should be enough.'

Flo nods and loads up a wheelbarrow, shepherd's hook over her arm like a modern Bo Peep.

'Hi!' says Jessie, brightening. 'Great to see you! Have yourself a bath,' she says, nodding at the stone trough that's filled ready for me with steaming water. Maeve drops in a muslin pouch and swooshes it around the tub with her hand. It smells of springtime. Lemon passes me a towel, and helps Maeve move a screen in front of the trough for privacy.

'Maybe one day you'll get here through an actual door, huh?'

'I should have explained about old Creepy Crawley,' says Flo, later, waiting as it takes me a beat to remember Lottie's very fitting surname. 'But when you and I saw her in the street, I thought you were Lemon.' She smiles, sheepishly. 'Sorry.'

'It's not just on you, Flo,' says Jessie. 'Any of us could – or should – have spoken to Nin about her.' She loops a hand round a clutch of braids and pushes them over her shoulder. 'After a couple of the girls said they were approached by her, I did a little digging.'

'Lottie approached more of you?'

Velvet pulls a purple-coloured necklace from her pocket. She explains that Lottie bought her tea 'in an actual tea shop', gave her the necklace and fed her the 'we're the same' line. Maeve has a similar story. Luckily, both girls were wary and didn't meet up with Lottie again.

I rip the necklace from my neck. 'Ugh, how *could* she?' *Damn you, Creepy Crawley.*

Jessie continues. 'Our team found this.'

*Our team?* There's a lot from the future that Jessie isn't telling us. She waves what looks like an ancient school exercise book. 'Arrest records. We already knew that Lottie's had a brush or two with the law, for petty theft among other things. But now we know who the arresting officer was –'

'Detective Simons?' I offer.

'The very same. But there's more. It was you talking about generations and passing things on, Nin, that got me thinking.'

I hear Lemon mutter 'swot' under her breath and I stick my tongue out at her.

'We went back a little further. Seems Lottie's mom was also no stranger to the inside of a cell.' She flicks through the arrest records and turns the book towards me. Among row after row of swirly, scratchy writing, an entry has been highlighted with a glowing yellow smudge.

*Dorothy Crawley, arrested and cautioned for aiding and abetting Rev. Silas Tate. Released into the care of Mr J. Bletchley, who also undertook to pay her good behaviour bond.*

I don't understand. 'Who are these people?'

'Dorothy — also known as Dotty — was Lottie's mom,' Jessie explains. 'She was a housemaid where Peggy Devona lived in Bristol.'

The mention of Peggy Devona sends shivers down my spine. 'Was that when Peggy saved her best friend from the hangman?' I rub at my own neck.

'Uh-huh,' says Jessie. 'Reverend Tate was the creep who manipulated Dotty into helping him.

He's the one who framed Peggy's friend. He also threatened to have Peggy thrown into an . . . well you call them lunatic asylums.'

'What an awful man,' I say. And how sad that Lottie's mother was taken in by him.

Jessie falls quiet. There's something else. 'Tate was one of the original members of The Righteous.'

Lemon lets out a low whistle. 'Like mother, like daughter.'

'Where are you, girls?' mutters Jessie, staring at a plan. 'OK, let's add the route we just took to find Nin to our map.' She says 'route' to rhyme with 'gout' and 'trout'. 'So, you think the pin factory, if that's what we're calling it, is just about here?' She points to an area off Longsmith Street.

'Yes,' I say, 'I think so.' I look more closely. 'What's that, there?' Directly behind the pin factory is Westgate Street. Seems I wasn't so lost after all. 'I felt prickles in my fingers when I stood outside the undertaker's on Westgate Street, too.' I lift up my glasses and almost press my nose to the paper. 'Yes! That would be it, right there! The pin factory is at the back of the undertaker's, it's the same building!'

They look so different; the rear of the building is a red-brick wall and plain, the front a picture-perfect, black-and-white Tudor merchant's house.

Jessie sits back on her haunches. 'Interesting. You know, there's talk of a secret underground tunnel running all the way from the docks to the cathedral.' She traces a finger over the map. 'You said there was a gap in the tunnel you were stuck in? To the left of you, before you fell?'

I nod. 'Yes, I'm pretty sure of it.'

'Maybe that leads to the secret tunnel between the cathedral and the docks. That gap's got to be there for a reason,' says Lemon. She sits beside me and rests her chin on my shoulder. 'Or it could just be Roman remains, like here.'

'I don't know,' says Jessie. 'I keep expecting to see a pattern, but it's random.'

I pull my gaze back from the map. There *is* something there, like when I looked at it before, but I can't quite join the dots. I'm so tired I can't think straight.

'How about we all try and get some sleep?' suggests Maeve. 'In the morning things may seem clearer.'

It's the best idea I've heard in forever.

The next morning the five of us try to formulate some sort of plan.

There are three separate issues: finding the rest of the missing whisperlings; foiling whatever Lottie and The Righteous are planning; and helping Wilf. Four issues, if you count retrieving the Book of Devona from the pin factory basement.

'It certainly feels like a lot to do,' says Maeve, nibbling on a fingernail. 'We'll have to share the missions out between us.'

She's right. Lemon wants to try and see Wilf at the gaol, but it's too risky. 'Detective Simons is behind Wilf's arrest, I'm sure of it,' I say, shaking my head. 'If he'd been arrested for Lemon's alleged murder, then we could've easily disproved it by showing up at the gaol. But he was arrested for going AWOL . . .' There is little we can do to help him at the moment, and every time I think about it my throat tightens.

Finding the missing whisperlings and foiling The Righteous are essentially the same mission, and Lottie is the key to both. Lemon seems optimistic about it. 'If we can get Lottie onside,' she says, 'there's a chance she could simply tell us everything they're planning and we could all be home by teatime.'

*Home.* The word clangs like a bell in my stomach. Whatever happens, Lemon and I must get back today to check on Mam, even if we then return to Gloucester once we've seen for ourselves that she's recovering. The thought that Mam might be more unwell than Bessie let on isn't something we've admitted out loud, but that fear sits between us like a snake in a box.

We decide it's only right to try and tell the parents of the missing girls about The Righteous, and our suspicions that they're keeping their children somewhere in Gloucester. The best way to do that – because telling the police is no longer an option – is to involve the brave women from the anti-war protest. 'There's usually a pocket of them outside the council building,' says Maeve, winding her hair round her hand like a bandage before putting it up on her head and fastening her hat over the top. 'I'm sure they'll know how to help. I'll ask them about Wilf as well.'

'Should we give them the names of The Righteous that we already know?' I ask. 'If the women know about Detective Simons and Dr Wibley and are anything like our mams, they'll find them and tear them limb from limb.'

'Well then, yes, of course!' says Flo. Lemon and I exchange a look. For a girl who looks like a delicate china doll, Flo definitely has a bloodthirsty side. They'd said in the newspaper she was a troublemaker, but I'm not entirely sure that's true either.

I take an opportunity later as we're sitting by the fire to ask Flo what her real story is. 'Me, a "troublemaker"? Don't know what they're on about,' she confirms with a smile. 'I was – *am* – a Girl Guide, and a bleedin' good one. Might 'ave got involved with the suffragettes, but I don't know why that's seen as a bad thing . . .'

The suffragettes are a group who are fighting to get women on an equal footing with men. The mams are keen supporters; we occasionally have meetings at the pub. But there are many women and girls involved in the movement so I can't see how that might cause The Righteous to single Flo out. When I mention this to her, she shrugs.

'Well, er, there *was* an incident at the Tower of London. Might've been that.'

'I remember reading about it!' I say. The suffragettes smashed the glass surrounding the crown jewels. There was a huge outcry, and it gave much publicity to the cause. Flo sees my reaction, a bit horrified but mostly impressed.

'Can't make an omelette without breaking a few eggs . . .' she remarks, then pauses. '. . . Or highly secured display cases on that particular occasion,' and I giggle along with her. Troublemaker or not, Flo is certainly brave.

'You're all girls who've drawn attention to yourselves in some way,' says Jessie, as the other creepers join us by the fire. 'Which made you more likely to be accused of being whisperlings, and any reports in the newspapers about you more negative, especially if it's a newspaper that The Righteous have any influence over.'

A chill runs down my spine. 'Just like in the witch trials,' I whisper. It was a subject we covered in one of our home-schooling lessons and was one of the few things both Lemon and I paid attention to. Back then, any woman seen as different or – heaven forbid! – *clever* could find herself accused of witchcraft and put to death.

'But how did they *know* we were whisperlings?' asks Maeve. 'Apart from you two, Clemmy and Nin – your messagings made it pretty obvious that you were creepers. But the rest of us were just –'

'A "bit much"!' interrupts Lemon, echoing the mean words I said to her when we rowed before she left. 'Isn't that right, Nin?'

'It certainly is. And isn't it brilliant,' I say, with a smile.

Velvet jabs at the dancing, spitting flames of the fire with a poker. A scarf, long, cream and knitted, swirls round her neck up to her nose like piped icing and she pushes it down to speak. 'How did it feel?' she says, putting the poker down and fixing me with cat-like, emerald eyes.

'How did *what* feel?'

'The book! When you held it.' She shuffles forward and so do the rest of them. Flo, cross-legged, rests her elbows on her knees and I feel like a teacher at story-time.

'Well,' I say, pushing my mind back to – oh my goodness, was it only yesterday? 'It was as if . . . you know at the seaside? And you're standing in the sea and the tide is on its way out and it pulls and pulls at yer legs like it's sucking you off yer feet? It was sort of like that, to start with. She – Lottie – keeps it in a locked drawer of a bureau, but I could feel it even through the wall when I took off my gloves.'

'How do you mean?'

'It called to me. Dragged me to it.' I sit back, a thought pulsing in my head. 'Was that it?' I say to myself as much as to anyone. 'The rift, I mean. Was that the book all along? When The Righteous stole it, or tried to use it, did the book . . . I don't know, *call* to us whisperlings?'

'Like a distress signal?' says Jessie. 'Wow, it really could have been.'

Perhaps we got it wrong, my sister and I. When the rift happened, we'd thought it was something to fear, that something terrible was coming to get us.

248

What if all along it had been a cry for help? A *rallying* cry?

'Oh my god, the book called us up!' says Flo. 'Like soldiers.'

'Yes. It created an army of creepers,' I whisper. I close my eyes to try and remember details. 'When I touched it, it was like it was part of me. It felt like when Lemon and I hold hands . . .' I slip off a glove and grab Velvet's hand; a fizz like static makes her jump.

'What was that!' she yelps, astonished.

I stop in my tracks. 'You don't know?' I thought *everyone* knew. 'It's a creeper thing. If you link hands with another creeper, it sort of boosts your powers. It's why Lemon and I do the messagings together, holding hands.'

'You have *got* to be kidding,' Velvet says. 'I presumed that was just a twin thing!'

'It's one of the first things we learned *not* to do too much. It can be a bit scary.'

Velvet narrows her eyes. 'The first thing *who* learns? Whisperlings? Or just *Devona* whisperlings?'

'Velvet, stop,' says Jessie with a smile. 'She's messing with you, Nin. *Of course* we all know that. How do you think we speak to our ghostly friends here?'

I flush, embarrassed, and Velvet winks at me. 'Sorry, Nin. Couldn't resist. Carry on, please.'

'When I touched the book, it was as if I was unlocking something.' I put my hands out, pretending the book is under my fingertips. 'It looks really old, the cover is leather and sort of puffy. Maybe it got wet and dried out –' I turn my hands over in front of me. 'Like my gloves.' I run my fingers over the imaginary cover, smiling as I remember how it felt. 'It felt as if we knew each other. Like family.' I imagine running a finger over the design that's embossed on the cover, the crude shape of an eye, the crown-like licks of the flames, so alive it made my fingers burn.

*The crude shape of an eye . . .*

'Oh my goodness.' I sit back with a jolt.

'What?' says Lemon. 'What is it?'

I slap my forehead with the back of my hand. 'I'm such an idiot! It's been in front of my face all along.' I jump to my feet. 'Where's the map?' I flap my hands, agitated.

Flo gets it out of her knapsack, passes it to me and, my hands shaking, I unfold it and spread it over the floor as the girls gather round. 'We've been looking at this wrong.' I jab at the map with my finger, tracing the dots of the 'ins' with my finger. 'See?'

The girls look at each other, confused. 'Pencil – pencil – pencil, pencil, pencil!' I jabber and with flustered fingers I quickly join up the dots on the map in the pattern I know it to be. Lemon slaps a hand to her mouth.

'I see it,' she whispers. 'Look.' She turns the map round.

'The locations of the entrances *aren't* random,' I explain, standing back to properly look. It couldn't be clearer; my hurried pencil marks have picked out a pattern. A beautiful, ancient, magical pattern. Made for us, by us. 'Look!' I say. 'Under the city lies a secret: a scattering of ancient catacombs, cellars and vaults, all threaded together by a web of tunnels and burrows. And the entrances to those tunnels?'

'It's in the shape of an eye,' whispers Jessie, tracing the pencil marks with her finger. 'Well, I'll be damned.'

'And this, here –' I tap at a point on the map, energy sparking from me – 'is the pupil.' The girls nod in agreement. 'That's where they are. The missing girls. I'm sure of it.'

I know it, I know it in my soul. The 'witch's hat' vision was more specific than I realized. And I *saw* it, with my own eyes. I'm such a fool. It wasn't the light of a thousand candles, illuminating the cathedral windows when I first arrived. It was the glow of countless missing whisperlings.

The missing creeper girls being held in Gloucester Cathedral.

36

Something is spreading into the city, a devilish, creeping darkness as suffocating and deadly as an oil spill. I can feel it.

A request to search the cathedral was dismissed, as expected. The suggestion that kidnapped girls were being held on sacred ground was met with horror, disbelief and the threat of the law.

There's only one other way. 'There's a tunnel between the docks and the cathedral,' Jessie had said and now, after studying the newly plotted map, there seems another place for this critical 'in'. An obvious place, where all would be welcome. A place of refuge.

Flo and I are focused – excited almost. The plan has changed; no longer do we need to rely on Lottie doing the right thing. We know where the missing girls are, and we're going to get them. We have rope and lamps and a pickaxe ('For tunnelling, or hitting villains over the head with, should the need arise,' said Flo, with disconcerting glee). The plan is to find the missing girls, and even if we can't get them to freedom we can get proof of their capture and alert the authorities.

'The police can't *all* be members of The Righteous, surely?' said Velvet, earlier. 'There must be *some* good ones?' She'd looked stricken, and I was quick to reassure her, even if I wasn't really as confident as I made out. The law-makers we've met seem to be very keen law-breakers, but I don't tell her this, especially as Lemon, Maeve and Flo have gone to hunt round the cathedral grounds for possible access.

Flo and I push on through the sideways rain. I try and ignore the water sluicing over the camber of the street, flushing out from overflowing drains and flowing over cobbles. *It isn't coming to get you*, I tell myself. *Don't be stupid*. When we get to the docks, it's chaos. Sandbags are piled up in a vain attempt to keep the water out, but it's too late for many of the warehouses. Water pushes over the lip of the basin and I remember a school science lesson, when we dropped coins into an already full glass and watched in fascination as the skin of the water stretched and held itself in a flattened sphere, above the rim.

Until it didn't.

My heart thuds. I've seen it before, fields covered by black water seeping outwards, greedily eating land and snapping at the heels of terrified, bleating, scattering sheep, river water pushing over the makeshift dam of the ships' graveyard, raising the canal, trapping the city in its watery, deadly claw.

We round the corner, and I see it. The single-storey, simple building that from a distance looks little more than a stone barn. The humblest of places of worship, with a direct line underneath it to one of the grandest.

'No,' I whisper, voice silent in the storm. The seafarers' chapel is surrounded by water, like a moat. 'No.'

We stand in silence. There's no way to get close enough to find the 'in', let alone enter it. I sink to my knees. Rain pummels my back, sliding down my waxy cape and soaking into the backs of my legs. My hands are *under* the water, but I no longer care. Water swishes over my gloves, the loose thread wafting in the current, and for a moment I am at the seaside, watching an anemone in a rock pool. I pull my hands out. My gloves are sea-slicked and loose, the outer seam almost totally unstitched, my skin bone-white against its black shroud. They're ruined. It doesn't matter.

My stomach twists in horror. I think of the map, the tunnel from here at the docks to the cathedral is now filling with water.

*The tunnel will flood. The girls under the cathedral will . . .*

I look at Flo; her stricken face tells me that she realizes it too. 'What do we do?' she asks.

I stand up, peel off my gloves and throw them in the swirling puddle.

'Whatever we have to.'


The pin factory is our only option now. The narrow tunnel from the bread oven is the only route left to us. I pray the others have found a different way. I am not sure this plan will work. What if Lottie doesn't let us in? What if we do get in and manage to crawl down the tunnel without getting stuck, but find that the other tunnel, the one that branches off to the left, *doesn't* lead to the cathedral?

As Flo and I draw closer, my neck prickles and it feels like something is sitting heavy on my chest. It reminds me of the legend of the night-hag, a wizened, veiled crone Lemon and I read about in an old book of Mam's. The hag scuttles from the gloom and settles on your chest as you sleep. And when you wake ... *you can't move.* She pushes pinching fingers into your mouth to hold your tongue to stop you screaming. She's so close you can see the hairs on her warts and the crusts in the corners of her eyes. You can smell the rotten, metallic tang of her breath but you *still* can't move. Night after night she sits on your chest until you give her your soul to end the torment. Bessie said it was just a folk tale and really the feeling is caused by your brain being half asleep, but I swear if I look down I'll see the night-hag clinging to my chest.

'I can barely see you,' says Flo. She's right; it's getting darker. I look up; once again there's movement against the lamplight, like a bullfighter agitating his cape. Some*thing* is shadowing the light.

My legs want to go the other way – the night-hag on my chest has two friends clinging to my ankles – but I force myself forward. The pin factory comes

257

into view, red brick darkened to the colour of blood by the rain. A pulse thuds in my temples as we tuck ourselves behind a low wall, out of sight. Breath catches in my throat; wispy, black spectres are swirling around the building, tendrilous and grabbing. My horror is reflected in Flo's face. When we link hands, she can see them, too, but neither of us want to let go.

It isn't just ghostly visitors: fancy motor cars line the road outside the building; in one, a chauffeur in a peaked hat and white gloves blows smoke out through a gap in the front window.

'Maybe it's just a party,' says Flo, with mock bravery. 'Can you hear that?' Crackling gramophone music oozes from an open window, the swirling wind throwing odd, fragmented melodies in our direction. I swallow. This is not a party I want to go to.

I glance up to the sky: the storm clouds churn with a strange, dark malevolence, other-worldly shrieks mixing with the hiss and roar of wind and rain. With a slap I realize why it all feels so familiar. That strange depth to the sky, suggesting a gateway through to somewhere else, somewhere dark . . . 'It's like the rift!'

Flo nods in agreement. 'Perhaps it *wasn't* the book calling us, then. Maybe it was those idiots in their so-called TR Society messing around with it.'

'Or maybe it was the book calling us *because* they were messing about with it? They're dabbling with stuff they don't understand.' With a shudder I remember the five-pointed star on the floor of the basement. *Just what are they doing in there?*

'That Lottie is such a traitor.' Flo is absolutely right. I still can't believe a whisperling would collaborate with our mortal enemies. 'A very *shiny* traitor.'

'Oh, this is hopeless.' I rest my forehead on the cold, wet brick. How on earth are we to get in and anywhere near the tunnel now? It was always going to be difficult, but now, with all of them in there . . . it's impossible. And Lottie's shine is *so* bright . . . she must be a really powerful whis— *Wait* . . .

'Flo . . . you called Lottie "shiny".'

'So? She *is* shiny.'

I grip her by the shoulder and pull back my hood. 'What do you see?'

Flo looks at me like I'm a tiger she's accidentally caught in a rat trap. 'Er, I see a strong and confide—'

'No, you plonker, what do you actually *see*, in my face?'

'Um, I see freckles, and a dimple –' she pokes me in the cheek – 'right there. And specs that've fallen down your nose.' Flo pushes my glasses back up my face. 'I see someone who is brave, even though they're scared. I see a soldier.'

Warmth pools in my tummy. But that isn't what I mean. 'But can you see anything else? Do I look shiny at all to you?'

'*Ohhh* . . . right, I'm with you now.' Flo tilts her head to one side and looks at me as if I were a painting in a museum. 'And whereabouts might it be, this shine of yours?'

She can't see it. Not every creeper can see another's shine.

And if she can't see mine, at all, how on earth could she have seen Lottie's?

37

'Could Lottie be faking it?' says Flo.

'I don't know,' I reply, 'maybe. But she *is* a whisperling – she saw the ghosts that came through when she made me lay my hands on the book.'

Or did she? I think back. She definitely reacted to that ratty, shredded phantom that landed on her shoulder, but she didn't react to the ghost children of the factory at all. I spool back to the previous evening. 'She gripped my arm,' I say, remembering how she stopped me from trying the basement door. 'And I didn't feel anything.' If she was as powerful a whisperling as she says she is, I'd have felt *some* connection, surely?

It feels like we've been out here for hours, on our bellies peering through the basement window of the pin factory, although it can only have been ten minutes or so. The ground is freezing and although my cape is good cover from the rain it isn't all that long and the backs of my legs are sodden and numb with cold. Inside, buttery-yellow flames dance and glitter; there must be a hundred candles down there, some gathered in groups as if huddling together for warmth, others set in a circle round the five-pointed star on the ground.

As well as Lottie, there are five men down there in the basement: Detective Simons, Dr Wibley and three others. They all have well-groomed moustaches or solid-looking, sculpted beards that look like they're carved from marble. All of them are dressed alike, in matching black floor-length tunics with wide bell sleeves, fringed scarves embellished with strange symbols like Egyptian hieroglyphs, and puffed-up headdresses made of striped material, like the pharaohs from my schoolbooks.

'What the Franz Ferdinand do they think they look like?' says Flo. 'I'm all for a drop of theatre, but that is taking the custard cream.'

On the back of each tunic is embroidered an interlinked T, T and R.

' "The The Righteous",' I whisper. Flo giggles, nervously.

In the basement, Lottie places the Book of Devona on a podium and I feel like I'm being sucked towards it by my chest. One of the robed men steps from the room and returns a moment later, dragging with him a girl with short, boyish hair. He throws her to the floor and she draws her knees to her ribs, curling up like a frightened hedgehog.

'They've got Lemon!' I whimper. 'Flo! Go get help!'

'Hang on – what are you going to . . . No, Nin, *no, no, no!*'

But I ignore her pleading and in one movement I'm up on my feet and running towards the door.

*Bangbangbangbangbang!*

'Let me in, let me in, let me IN! I know you have my sister!' As soon as Lottie opens the door I throw myself to my knees and grip the skirts of her robe. Meanwhile, Flo is crouched behind a motor car with her hands clamped over her mouth. '*Go!*' I mouth at her and she nods, and skitters off.

'Both of you? We have *both* of you?' Lottie claps her hands as if she's been given a box of puppies. 'Ooh, they are going to *love* me for this!'

'I'm begging you, I know you're going to tell them about me, but please, please give me five minutes to explain. I think I know where the missing girls are, and they're in danger. And so are you, Lottie. *Please.*'

'And you've just *presented* yourself to me . . . just like that!' She looks upwards and whispers a prayer of thanks. 'The spirits really *are* aligned tonight,' she says, eyes gleaming with delight. She flicks a look to the closed basement door, behind which loud, male voices guffaw and bray and cigar smoke seeps out round the edges like a rolling smog. The maid passes us in the hallway, scowling and muttering bitterly about 'manners'. Lottie doesn't acknowledge her.

Here, under the custardy glow of paraffin lamps, Lottie's skin is silvery, like a fish on a slab in the market. But when she tucks a stray wisp of hair behind her ear, I can see her jaw is swollen.

'Five minutes,' she says, brushing my dirty handprints from her robe with a grimace. 'And don't try anything funny –' she glowers at me – '*this* time.'

I tell her about the tunnel, and how it's likely to be flooded by now. I tell her how we saw mothers, parents at the anti-war protest, begging for help to find their whisperling daughters. I explain how The Righteous have manipulated people before, how it's easy to be carried along by lies when you're feeling a bit lost. I say everything I can think of to make her help me.

And then when that doesn't work, I beg. I beg her to let Lemon go, to do it for me; I beg her to do it for the mams – when I mention them, her face scrunches up as if she's working out a really difficult sum, and the swelling on her jaw reddens. I rub at my cheek, her puffy face reminding me of when Lemon and I had mumps and had to hold stinky hot poultices to our faces, which made us gag.

'You said your mam had passed,' I say, trying anything that might get through to her. 'What happened to her?'

'Mammy was a grafter, but that didn't get 'er nowhere.' She speaks quickly as if she wants to get the story over with, her soft accent and dainty way of talking hardening as she speaks. 'Had a right chip on 'er shoulder. She was a whisperling, you know. A crap one, but still. Didn't do 'er any good. I vowed never to make the same mistake. Looked out for meself all me life – no one else will.'

'And what about you?' I ask. 'What sort of whisperling are you?' and I'm about to add *apart from a treacherous one* when there is a puff of rottenness and darkness swirling and swishing round my head like the belching fumes of a motor car.

'Don't listen,' it rasps, its blackened mouth gaping and drooling like a spilling bucket of tar. 'She is the enemy! We, *The Righteous*, are your true family!' The phantom creature settles on Lottie's frame like a rancid bird and although it must be weightless her shoulder lowers a fraction.

'You can hear it?' I ask. 'You can hear that blob talking to you?' It seems denser in form than before. *Can it be gaining in strength, somehow?* The thought makes me shudder.

'It isn't an *it*, it's a *he*,' she corrects me with a glare. 'Yes, I can.' Perhaps the spectre on Lottie's shoulder is the ghost of the man who used her mother. It would explain how it – he – knows about Devona whisperlings.

'Since when? Have you always been able to hear him?'

She shakes her head. 'Only since Mam passed. It was the one useful thing she left me.' She juts out her chin in tiny, misplaced triumph. 'Got louder after that thing happened. *The rift*, or whatever you call it.'

'It's using you, and The Righteous are using you too, Lottie,' I say gently. 'They're planning something awful. You only have to look at the sorts of spirits surrounding the building to know that.'

'There are spirits surrounding the building?'

'You can't see them?'

'Of course I can!' she lies, flicking her hair from her face. 'I was just testing you.'

I glance round at the countless harmless, wispy souls milling about us, echoes of people that have lived in this ancient building. She can't see any of them. Just that horrible, mean one on her shoulder.

'Please, Lottie, help me get Lemon out of here. Let's put a stop to this! These people are not your friends.'

' "Friends"?' Lottie snarls, throwing her arms out wide. 'Who, exactly, are my *friends*? Are they the poshos Ma worked for all her life who I wasn't good enough for? Are they your little creeper chums who think they're so special they won't play with me even when I give them jewellery?'

'But you didn't want to *play*, Lottie.' She squirms at the repetition of her childish phrase and in that moment it's obvious that she isn't a young lady, she's a girl, a little girl, in a stupid, too-grown-up dress. 'You wanted to use them to make you feel important.'

The basement door opens. Detective Simons steps through a cloud of grey cigar smoke, wagging his hands like a conjurer stepping on to a stage.

268

'Well, well, what do we have here, then?' His voice is as big and round and loud as a church bell. 'I thought I sensed something in the ether,' he says. 'And look! The gods have brought us the other one!' He flicks Lottie a disdainful look. 'Let's see if you've *finally* come up with the goods, shall we?'

He makes a grab for me, but my cape is slick from the rain and I slip away from him. He lunges, gripping me tightly round the middle, squeezing the breath from my gut. 'Scrappy little so-and-sos these freaks, ain't they?' he says, hauling me off like a bundle of washing under his arm.

Lottie watches on, squishing her lips together with her fingers. There's one last thing I could try.

'I'll help you see her!' I croak, breath ragged.

Lottie's eyes snap to my face. 'What?' she says, years falling from her. 'Who d'you mean?'

'I can do it. You were right. I'll help you see her,' and then a rag is over my mouth and I can't breathe, I can't breathe, and the last thing I see is Lottie, her expression unreadable, with that smiling ghoul dragging her down as if it weighs a ton.

Lemon, hands tied behind her back, sits to the right of me in the middle of the pentagram. A bruise blooms above her eye. She catches me looking.

'You know me, I don't take well to being told what to do,' she says with a shrug.

'How did they get you?'

'I went to see Wilf.'

'Lemon! We said you mustn't –'

'I know, *I know*,' she interrupts, 'but I felt so bad for him I wanted to tell him we were trying to get him out and, well, anyway. It was a trap. One of The Righteous' goons was there, waiting.' She slides her eyes to a shadowy corner. 'There's a couple of 'em in here, standing guard.'

'Oh Lemon.' I shuffle to her side, hip sore where

I landed on the floor. I put my head on her shoulder. 'It'll work out all right. We'll get out of this, together, somehow.'

Lottie lights a circle of candles round us, moving swiftly, waving the taper like a conductor's baton. The basement room has been swept and polished, the walls freshly limewashed and dressed with pictures of these well-fed, well-groomed men, all looking very pleased with themselves.

'I love what you've done with the place,' I say, but Lottie ignores me. Her eyes flick to Lemon's bruise and she swallows.

'Be quiet,' says Lottie between clenched teeth. 'Just do as they say, perform the ritual and this will all be over with.'

'What "ritual"?' Lemon scoffs.

'And then what, Lottie?' I say. 'They'll chuck us in a pit under the cathedral, with the others? Hopefully, it hasn't flooded yet because they'll be chucking you down there, too, you see if they don't.'

'Shut up, both of you, just shut up!'

'I tried,' whispered Lemon when Lottie is out of earshot. 'They made me put my hands on the book and I really concentrated and it tingled but I couldn't get anything to happen.' She shrugs. 'I don't know what they were expecting, but it wasn't good enough for them.'

The Book of Devona is open on the podium, displayed like an ancient manuscript in a museum. I felt it immediately, that invisible thread stitching us together. There's movement at the edges of my vision too; shadows skin from the walls, quietly rolling and tumbling towards us like a silent tide.

'You're wrong,' I murmur to Lemon. 'You *did* do something. Look!' Something else is here. Something that hangs in the air like sparkling dust motes, tiny stars fallen from the sky. I've seen them before. When I fell into the canal, in the docks, even in the puddles in the city. They were always there, trying to help. I just didn't realize it. But now it's unmistakable. It's *never* felt as powerful as this. Energy crackles from them like tiny firecrackers.

'Someone heard you,' I tell her.

'Who?' she asks. 'I didn't . . . oh my goodness!' She gasps. 'I see them, I see them! What *are* they?'

'I'm not sure,' I whisper. 'But I think, between you, you and the Book of Devona called for the cavalry.'

*

'He looks like Frankenstein's monster,' whispers Lemon nodding towards one of the robed men. He's sallow-faced with eyes like pale moons, his head the same width as his neck.

'Or a thumb,' I whisper back, but when I look at him more closely I realize I recognize him from one of the newspapers. 'It's the mayor!'

The men all look ridiculous. They refer to each other as 'brother', and to Detective Simons as 'Grand Guru'.

Detective Simons – Grand Guru – claps his hands. 'Welcome, welcome, to our guests of honour. You are, young creepers –' at this, Lottie bristles – 'about to witness a miracle. 'Tis a shadowy boundary between life and death. Who knows where it begins and ends? Tonight, we shall see.' He waves an arm in a flourish.

I recognize the quote he's mangling. 'It's: *The boundaries which divide Life from Death are at best shadowy and vague. Who shall say where the one ends, and where the other begins?*' I correct him, and Lemon's eyes widen in surprise.

A vein pulses in the detective's forehead. 'A fan of Edgar Allan Poe, I see.'

'One of my mams likes him.'

He raises an eyebrow. 'You and your *mams*. How bohemian.' He chortles, looking round the room, his expression a cattle-prod to encourage the others to laugh.

'Right, brothers.' He walks over to the podium. 'Let's give it another go, shall we? Oh no, that really won't do!' He huffs, like a stroppy toddler and holds a hand to his eyes. 'It's too bright in here. Would someone douse a candle or ten?' He squints towards Lottie. 'Be a love.'

She does as she's bid, taking up the long-handled snuffer with its little cone and extinguishing some of the candles. Looks are exchanged behind her back, childish smirks and rolled eyes. *They're laughing at her.* Ridiculously – because why should I feel sorry for her? – I feel offended on Lottie's behalf.

With the light dimmed, the basement is now bathed in an eerie glow. Symbols radiate from the walls as if written in flame. Lottie's shine is disturbingly bright. She bites down on her bottom lip and her teeth flare like a lit match. I look from her to the wall symbols, and back again. What am I missing?

Detective Simons skims through the Book of Devona until he finds what he's looking for. The pages defy him and refuse to lie flat. He lifts the book to crack the spine, with a noise like snapping bone. I flinch – what psychopath would do that to *any* book, let alone one so important? Simons takes a theatrical breath, widens his palms and places them down on to the open pages of the book. A feeling of nausea swishes in my stomach. He shouldn't be touching that –

'*You* shouldn't be touching that!' shouts Lemon.

Simons looks up, surprised. 'I beg your pardon?'

'*Shhh*, Lem,' I warn, swivelling my head to look at her. 'These are bad people. He might be in the police, but it makes no difference, you can't –'

'He shouldn't! He doesn't know what he's doing.'

Simons tilts his head, sneering like an amused snake. '*Pfft!* It's hardly difficult.' He pulls himself up to his full height and speaks as if performing in a play. 'My powers will open the dark portal through which our ancestors will come and bestow us with the gifts of prophesy and divination, rendering your kind irrelevant.'

'It actually says that?' I shuffle round to look up at him, like he's a teacher taking assembly in school. 'Where? Where does it say that?' There's no way the book would give instructions for something so hateful and dangerous to whisperlings.

'Absolute load of crap,' mutters Lemon, and I throw her a warning glance. 'And if you're so amazing then why do you need *us* to be here?'

'It's my interpretation of the text,' Simons replies loftily, 'which is *obviously* correct. Having a creeper present and using the incantation in the book is the best way to rid your kind of powers.'

'I can't tell you how long we've been waiting for this moment,' pipes up the toadying Dr Wibley. 'And to have two Esmonds here – what luck! None of the creepers we've tried this on before has been the right sort, have they, Grand Guru?'

'That's right, Brother Wibley.' Simons smiles a tight smile. 'Thank you for the clarification. It's true that we've been searching a long time for a half-decent specimen –' Lemon nudges me and I swallow – 'to enable a smooth transfer of abilities.'

'And now we've got two,' mutters one of the other 'brothers' under his breath, 'which no doubt will cost us twice as much.'

'You're *paying* him to make you a creeper?' Lemon says. There is a shuffle of feet and mutters of 'No!', 'Absolutely not!' and 'Nothing of the sort!'

'But you *are*, aren't you?' I say. 'If our abilities transfer to you, then you'll be creepers. Or whisperlings, whichever word you prefer. You'll literally become the thing you say you hate,' I add.

'No, silly girls.' Simons' face has taken on a purplish tinge. 'My brethren and I will not be *whisperlings*, limited to passing on trivial messages from dead nobodies. We will seek out the important dead. Scholars. Poets. Bankers. Men with something important to say.' He raises an eyebrow and rubs his hands together. '. . . Bank robbers . . . pirates –' a chuckle flutters round the room – 'anyone with something *interesting* to get off their chest. Who knows who we may communicate with!' He pauses, and points a finger theatrically around the circle. 'This ritual will also give me – *us*,' he corrects himself, 'the ultimate knowledge. We want to know what happens after we die, and, with that information, perhaps we shall even learn how to stop death itself. We shall become, in a word, invincible.'

'No whisperling knows that stuff, it isn't allowed!' I cry.

'Isn't *allowed*?' he sneers. 'Perhaps that's because until now no *man* has asked. So, no, we won't be "whisperlings", for that is nonsense for women. We shall be The Righteous! The Righteous, but with powers to elevate us beyond God.'

The collective intake of breath is audible and sharp. 'Steady on, old boy,' says one robed man, crossing himself so hurriedly that he knocks his headdress off-centre, where it remains at a jaunty angle.

'That does sound a bit blasphemous,' adds Dr Wibley, cautiously.

'Well, to me, it still sounds *a lot* like you want to be whisperlings.' Lemon smirks.

'That's enough from you,' says Simons. He runs a finger across his throat, and then turns and runs the same finger under the lines of some text in the Book of Devona. I hate him touching it; it's like a stab to the heart.

'You've got it wrong,' I say, voice thick with tears. 'None of that's meant for you. You don't understand it.'

He fixes me with a jeering glare. 'Oh? How difficult can it be?' he says, flicking the pages dismissively. 'For is not the entire book made up of the mere ramblings of women?'

The 'Grand Guru' circles the group, muttering meaningless affirmations to each man before pulling a slip of material from his sleeve like a magician.

'Today we are without sight, but tomorrow we shall see,' he intones as he blindfolds each of them in turn.

I lock eyes with Lottie and raise an eyebrow. She gives the tiniest shrug. She *knows* this is all nonsense! But she allows herself to be blindfolded, too, nonetheless. The ghoul appears at her shoulder, still gruesome but more human-shaped than before, a flash of white collar at its sinewy neck. It had instructed Lottie to keep the book safe, *until it's time*. Is *this* what it's been waiting for? Using this farce of a ritual to make himself stronger?

'You may experience some strange sensations,' Simons explains. 'But it is important you remain blindfolded, brothers, for the sights will be too much for you. I shall channel the psychic storm, at *great* danger to myself.' At this I roll my eyes. 'One word from either of you girls, and it'll be the last thing you ever say,' he hisses so close to my face I can smell the brandy on his breath.

He returns to the podium and, in spite of his audience being blindfolded, opens his arms wide like a posturing seagull.

'Let us begin. Ogethertay . . . oreverfay. Oreverfay ogethertay. Ogethertay oreverfay, oreverfay ogethertay.'

'What the . . .?' I know these words. It's *our* language, my sister's and mine, our secret, silly language. How is it in the Book of Devona, *how*? Next to me, Lemon's shoulders shake. I nudge her to stop laughing. 'Shush, Lem, they're not messing about!'

'Ogethertay oreverfay. Oreverfay ogethertay. Ogethertay oreverfay, oreverfay ogethertay.'

As he reads, the gramophone churns into life, the needle scratching painfully on the record as it turns, slowly at first and then faster, faster, the music wailing banshee-like in the small space.

'Ogethertay oreverfay. Oreverfay ogethertay. OGETHERTAY OREVERFAY, OREVERFAY OGETHERTAY!'

His voice rises with the increasing volume of the music. He reaches into his sleeve –

*Crack, crack-a-crack-crack!*

The 'brothers' gasp and whimper and Lemon snorts with laughter. 'They were firecrackers!' she shouts. 'You're being conned! This is no better than the seances in town. Why don't you all just go and see Blythe Bobbety or whatever her name is at the New Inn?'

'Ignore her, brothers!' Simons commands. 'Don't

280

let this devil's handmaid steer you from our path, for tonight, gentlemen, is the beginning of a new dawn for The Righteous!'

'Tomorrow!' yells Lemon. My shoulders hitch to my ears. *Please be quiet, please be quiet, please be quiet!*

'I beg your pardon?'

'Tomorrow. It will be dawn tomorrow, not tonight. You lot are so stupid!'

'I hope it *is* tonight,' says one of the brothers. 'I need some of that buried treasure to replace the money I've spent on this!'

There is a flicker of a smile at the edge of Simons' lip. Lemon sees it, too.

'What are you doing this for, Detective Simons?' she asks. 'Money? Fame?'

'Someone shut her up, will they?'

One of the men pulls down his blindfold and grabs at Lemon's bound arms, dragging her to the side of the room. 'Get OFF me!' she shouts, kicking and struggling.

'Stop it!' I yell, finally wriggling my hands free from the rope they'd used to tie me. 'Stop it! You're hurting her!'

'Shove her in the trunk!' commands Simons. 'I'm sick of this!'

Lemon is grabbed by her legs and arms and she writhes and kicks, twisting her body like a washrag. 'No!' she yells. 'Get off me –'

*Thud.*

The sound is like a cannonball falling on to sand.

It's a sound I'll forever hear, over and over and over.

'You dropped 'er,' I say, flatly. 'You dropped 'er on 'er head.' I scramble to her side. 'Lemon? Clemency?' I shake her shoulders. There is no movement. I lift her hand and it falls with a limp slap on the cold floor. 'You've killed 'er.'

My sister is dead.

The rest of the men remove their blindfolds.

'I'm a doctor,' says Wibley. 'Let me see her,' but he's blocked by Simons. 'Get out of my way, man! What are you doing?'

'I've waited half a lifetime,' says Simons. 'We are finishing this. You,' he says, pointing to me. 'Get here.' But I won't move away from my sister. I stay there, cradling her head in my hands.

Like speckles of sunshine through trees, twinkling, ancient spirits gather round us, waiting. Is this what they came for? To greet Lemon? Grief burns in my chest, a pure, white light of pain and fury.

Simons returns to the podium and cricks his neck. 'Right, where were we?'

Bewilderment rolls from the gathering like a shaken eiderdown.

'You can't be serious?' says one.

'Come on, Simons, this is preposterous. We can't –'

'Be quiet! None of you will be leaving anyway until this is done and you've paid me my fee. We can sort this mess out after that. And are you forgetting we still have to sort out all the others, too? Come, come, brothers – don't look so alarmed. You all knew this was coming.'

*The others.* Though my grief is a heavy shroud, weighted with boulders, I still have to do something.

'Right,' says Simons again, with a tight smile. 'Where were we?'

This time, I whisper the words along with him.

'Ogethertay oreverfay. Oreverfay ogethertay. Ogethertay oreverfay, oreverfay ogethertay.'

'And now, little freak,' he says with a sneer, 'it's your moment.'

'Believe nothing you hear, and only one half that you see,' I say.

'What?'

'It's another Edgar Allan Poe quote. Mam's favourite. Appropriate for you,' I say, taking a step forward. 'But not for me.'

I place my hands on the Book of Devona. Energy rushes into me. 'Ogethertay oreverfay. Oreverfay ogethertay. Ogethertay oreverfay, oreverfay ogethertay.'

'What do you think you're doing?' He grabs my wrist but my arm won't budge; my hands are locked to the pages. Ribbons of energy thread themselves around me and the room shakes as the men's portraits clatter from the walls, first one, then another and another, flung across the basement like cards flicked from a pack as the men cry out, their voices shrill with fear.

'Is it an earthquake, Papa?' stammers one of the robed figures. *Papa?* He's little more than a boy, and a scared one at that. With a jolt I recognize him as one of the posh lads who mocked me in the alley on my first day in the city.

'*Boo*,' I say, and he skitters backwards on his bottom like a giant has flicked him away and covers his head with his robe, whimpering.

'Stop it!' shrieks Dr Wibley.

I ignore him. I couldn't stop now even if I wanted to. 'Ogethertay oreverfay. Oreverfay ogethertay. Ogethertay oreverfay, oreverfay ogethertay.'

There is a flash in my heart, and a feeling of pressure, like a fissure in a rock giving way to the relentless push of water. It pours in, filling the emptiness in my chest.

'Ogethertay oreverfay. Oreverfay ogethertay. Ogethertay oreverfay, oreverfay ogethertay!'

Faster and faster I repeat the incantation, over and over and over, using the proper words now, our silly little hide-and-seek rhyme. 'Together forever. Forever together. Together forever. Forever together. Together forever. Forever together. Where are you, Lemon? Where are you?'

I open my eyes and, just like that, there she is.

41

This is our last moment together. A small, quiet pause as we hold hands pretending all is well, that we can't see, beyond the strange, gauze-like bubble we find ourselves in, our real selves surrounded by greedy, jealous men, one of us lying cold in the middle of a five-pointed star.

My sister smiles and squeezes my hand and I tell myself *Remember this, remember how it feels, remember the pressure of her fingers on your skin, how her nose crinkles when she's teasing you, remember laughing until you can't speak, remember being completely, utterly loved, remember never feeling alone.*

We haven't got long; my 'real' body is dragging my spirit back into it like quicksand.

Panic gallops at me. 'I could come with you!'

'No,' she says. 'It isn't your time.' She's so calm, almost ethereal already; a gentle, sunny glow surrounds her, like shimmering heat on a hot day.

'And nor is it *yours*!' I wail, because how could it be? She's twelve years old! A sister, a daughter, a friend . . . a whisperling.

A thought . . .

'Can't you stay?' I whisper. 'Somehow?'

'Maybe,' she says, in the same tone she always used when asked to do something that she definitely wasn't going to do. She puts a hand to my cheek. 'But don't worry, I'm not going, not just yet. We've got work to do. Come on.' She drags me to my feet. 'You need to get back down there and stop this. You've got to find the other girls, Nin.'

I feel scared, looking from her to down there, which now seems miles away, like I've climbed the tallest tree in the world without realizing. 'How?'

She gently swings my hands in hers from side to side. 'We jump, Nin. We jump.'

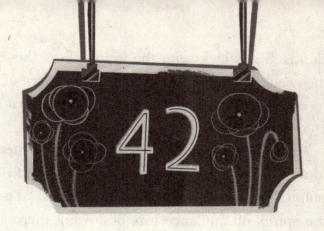

'What are you doing?' hisses Detective Simons, snatching the book from me. 'Who are you talking to?'

'Hey!' Lemon's ghost sparks in annoyance. 'Get off my sister!' She knocks him backwards with a firm shove to the chest and, his face scrunched with confusion, he stumbles, dislodging his headdress, which tumbles to the floor. There is a *clonk* and a *whizz* and a sound like a fishing rod being cast, as a swathe of black gauze descends from the ceiling towards the 'brothers', catching them, trembling and squirming, like mackerel in a net.

Lemon throws her arms wide and twirls like a top, her clothes billowing, incense vapours and candle smoke swirling round the basement like scudding clouds. She knocks into the gramophone, sending the needle skittering across the waxed surface of the record. It sounds like a pack of hyenas thrown into an orchestra pit.

'For goodness' sake,' mutters Simons, straightening himself up to address the room like a priest from a pulpit. 'Brothers, do not fear!' he intones. ''Tis but the spirits of our ancestors bestowing themselves upon you!' He reaches into his voluminous sleeve and pulls out a pot of glowing, sickly-smelling liquid, which he flicks with a stick on to the men, two of whom are still floundering on the floor in fright. 'Stay strong, brothers! The incantation is complete! By tomorrow, my brethren, we shall have the gift of sight!'

'Why tomorrow?' asks one of them. 'Why not now? We're sick of these delays, Simons. You've had us bring in girls from all over because none of them are ever right.'

Detective Simons ignores him. He rolls up the black gauze, shoves it in a bucket in the corner of the basement, picks up his headdress, returns to the podium and pulls a small box of matches from his sleeve. He removes one from the box and strikes it. Then, shielding the flame in his hand, he bends down to the floor. Sprinkled round the painted star is a fine trail of what looks like breadcrumbs. He puts the lit match to it and –

*Poof!*

It catches fire immediately, but the flames are not uniform. In the time since the 'crumbs' were carefully laid, the circle has been disturbed by tramping feet and flailing bodies.

Nothing is going as planned.

'What is that?' says one of the men, pointing at an eerily glowing patch on his robe.

'It's on all of you,' says Simons. 'Rejoice, brothers, for that is the whisperling glow. We have been blessed!'

But then . . .

'I'm on fire!' shrieks a man. He pulls off his robe and stamps on it but that only seems to make the flames more angry. As he hops from one foot to the other the flames unfurl, spreading and following the trail of scattered crumbs like a hungry hell-chicken, and soon there are little blazes everywhere. The bucket filled with the black gauze bursts into flames too, spitting sparks upwards, catching tinder-dry packing cases.

'We have to get out of here,' yells Lottie. 'It's going to blow!'

'What is?'

'That!' She gestures to an enamel pot containing a white, waxy substance. 'It's phosphorous.'

'Phosphorous?' The stuff they dip match-heads into, that can glow in the dark and . . . *Ohhh.* Lottie's strange, other-worldly glow, her swollen jaw . . . 'Lottie, *no*! Is that what you've been using on your face? But it's so dangerous!'

'I know.' Lottie puts a hand to her cheek, flinching as she scratches at her skin, leaving pinky-grey tracks in the fake lustre. 'I've lost some teeth, too,' she says, wiping at her eyes with her sleeve. The phosphorous leaves a silvery trail on her dress, as if it's been skated over by a family of snails. I want to hug her, but there's no time.

'Go!' Lemon's ghost grips me by the shoulders and although I shouldn't feel it I really can. 'Get to the cathedral, to the Creeper Gang . . . You've got to help them save the missing girls! Please, Nin!'

I shake my head. How can I possibly leave my sister here?

'Think of it as my last request,' she says with a cheeky smile.

'That's a low blow, Clemmy.'

'Lemon,' she says, fading slightly. 'My name is Lemon. Now please, Nin!' She starts to slip away from me.

With tears in my eyes, I turn to see Lottie being shoved backwards by that horrible, demonic ghoul on her shoulder. Then Lemon's ghost suddenly grabs it from Lottie's neck and throws it to the floor, where it rears up like a rattlesnake. I shove past Lottie who's mesmerized by the ghoul, her face a mixture of distress and relief and –

*Smash!*

The basement window shatters and – *whoomph!* – the fire flares with the rush of oxygen. I cover my face and fall to the floor. Someone outside shouts, 'Get back!' and a rush of water shoots over me and jets round the room like a scribbling pen.

Flo must have got help! Huzzah!

'Nin! GO!' shouts Lemon's ghost, pointing to the door of the old bread oven and for a minute I think Lottie is going to stop me; but no, she stands in front of me, shielding me from view, although no one is looking my way and Detective Simons is nowhere to be seen.

'Good luck,' she says, closing the door behind me with a thud and clunk.

I scooch down into the bread oven and push off into the darkness. This time, with my hands out in front of me, I can use my elbows and I know what's coming, and I make faster progress, even pushing through the extra earth the girls used to disguise the route. I'm going so quickly that when I get to the edge of the drop I almost go over, teetering like a seesaw into the void. Heart thumping, I stretch an arm to my left and I exhale in relief; I *hadn't* imagined it: there is a tunnel going that way.

It's easier to manoeuvre into than I'd thought. It goes on and on and, as I crawl into the gloom, I realize I'm heading downwards. There's that *fzzzz* sound again, growing louder this time. It's water, definitely. An underground stream, perhaps? Or could it be —

'Whoa!' The ground falls away, but for once I manage to stop myself from getting another bump on the head. I shift about so I'm sitting on the edge of the chute, legs dangling into the void. Water swooshes below, at least a foot high.

Flood water. And it's rising.

43

'It's all right,' I say out loud to reassure myself, but it isn't, it isn't all right at all. Panic charges at me like a lion. Water. Swooshing, rushing, *dangerous* water. 'I can wade through that,' I tell myself, trying not to look down.

With wobbly arms, I wriggle out of the chute, easing myself down until I have no choice but to let myself drop. What if this tunnel is deeper than all the others and the water goes over my head? I hold my breath – *splosh* – and when my feet touch solid ground I exhale, relieved. The water only comes up to my knees. For now.

I press both hands against the tunnel wall. Images flash in my vision, but I can't make them out. Fear punches my chest. Is it *my* fear, or fear from whatever

I'm feeling through my hands? I wade through the freezing water, running my fingers along the wall as I go. It feels like I'm wearing the leaded boots of a diving suit and as I push on, the water is harder to walk through, as if it's turning to ice around my legs.

*Push, push, push.*

To my horror, the tunnel slopes down once more and the water rams the backs of my numb, shaking legs, knocking my feet from under me. Panic pummels at my chest, momentum takes me, and I surge forward and then –

'*Ow!*'

I put my hands out in front of me. A wall. It's entirely solid, but how could this be here? For one thing, this space would be entirely filled with water by now, but . . . I pause, deliberately slowing my breathing, noticing it move up and down my body like Bessie taught me when I get myself in a pickle.

The bottom half of my body is still being dragged by the water. Moving slowly, I shuffle along the wall from left to right until my legs buckle forward. There's a *gap*. I run my hands down the wall, mapping it out and trying to ignore the panic snapping at me like a crocodile. It's *definitely* a gap, hip height and about the same measurement wide. A crawl space. But how far does it go?

I can't possibly risk it! I try to take a few steps back the way I came, but the water pushing against me is too strong; besides, how would I get back up to the higher levels of the tunnels with no ladder and no help? Tears prickle my eyes – *I'm going to drown, I'm going to drown* – and, as much as I want to be with my sister in the place she's gone, I'm scared. So I scream and scream and SCREAM.

'*Help us!*'

Wait – was that a shout? I stop screaming and listen, but it doesn't come again. I put my ear as close to the water by the crawl space, without dunking my head under, and listen again.

'*Is there anybody there?*'

'*Flo?* Is that you?'

'*Nin?* Is that you?'

'Yes, yes, it's me!' I'm crying and laughing. 'How long is the crawl space? Can I get through?'

'Yes, push yourself off and we'll grab you!'

I put my hands flat to the wall. With Flo touching it on the other side, it lights up like a bonfire.

I can do this. I can do this. *I have to do this*. I take my glasses off and put them in my pocket, take a breath, hold my nose and dive under the water.

Hands grab me and pull me spluttering and coughing to the surface on the other side.

'Oh my goodness, Nin! Is that really you?' Maeve has lost her hat. Standing in this cave, red hair tumbling to her hips with the water lapping around her, she looks like a mermaid. 'You'll catch your death if you stay like that! Here.' She peels off one of her layers, helps me out of my wet things and pulls a jumper over my head.

'Th-thank you.' I shiver, squeezing out my sodden hair as Maeve shakes off my cape and places it round my shoulders. My legs are blocks of ice but the rest of me is now surprisingly warm. That, or numb. I peer into the dark. 'What is this place?'

'Catacombs, we think. Deep under the cathedral's crypt. The Righteous goons that threw us in here had a key to some sort of secret entrance. We've screamed and shouted but . . .' Maeve shrugs and glances upwards at the cathedral above us. 'Nothing.'

'How would The Righteous even know this was down here?'

'They get everywhere, that lot,' says Velvet with a glower. 'Like cockroaches. Grabbed us as we were scouting out the cathedral – maybe they'd got wind we were poking about.' She nibbles at a blue-painted nail. 'There was a cover over that crawl space you came through, before the pressure of the water popped it open.' She points to a wooden door floating nearby. 'Otherwise we'd have tried to escape through there earlier. Water's been rising in here for the last couple of hours.'

'Before The Righteous grabbed me,' says Flo, 'I called in at the fire station, said all them candles at the pin factory were a hazard. Showed them my Girl Guide's safety badge.' She mimes flashing open her jacket like a crook selling stolen watches. 'Did it work?' She smiles, hopefully. 'Is help on its way?'

I can't answer. I scrub at my eyes with the heel of my hand and retrieve my glasses from my pocket and put them on. Light blooms on the smeary, water-dripped lenses and I rub to clear them with my fingers.

'Oh, my . . .'

There must be fifty girls down here, huddled together on ledges and outcrops. Whisperlings.

Creepers. Shining like the glow of a thousand church candles.

'Is everyone all right?'

'Mostly,' says Flo. 'We don't know yet what The Righteous were planning to do with them. With *us*. There are rumours of us being sent abroad, maybe into service. Maybe that's why Jessie thought –' she lowers her voice – 'that there were no survivors, in her future. Perhaps there were no records? Jessie *must* be wrong. They wouldn't just let us all die down here, would they?' She looks at me, hopefully. 'Besides, she said we –' she gestures at the four of us – 'and Lemon survive . . . And if *we're* in here with these girls, then surely everyone else will survive, too. Right?' She looks behind me. 'Where *is* Lemon?'

It's hard to form the words, but I have to. I take a breath and –

'Wait,' says Velvet. 'Can you hear that?'

A strange, low wind blows towards us, like the hot waft of a steam train racing through a tunnel.

There is movement under my feet: a shuddering, buzzing vibration, and I turn into the squall, hands out as if to deflect a blow.

'Get back!' I yell. 'Get up to safety!' Churning water is up to my knees and it spits and bubbles as if it's boiling. Ghouls surge into the cave, ripped from the murky edges of the veil by those stupid, power-hungry men.

I can't believe it. Is that idiot man Detective Simons still chanting?

'Come on, Nin, get up here!' The girls have climbed on to a ledge, and Flo and Velvet each grab one of my arms to haul me up and we crush ourselves backwards against the roughly hewn stone of the catacomb wall.

'This is bad,' says Flo. 'Really bad. There's no way out, unless we can get up there.' She nods to a spot even higher above us. It's like pointing to the top of a cliff. 'There's a ladder, but they pulled it up after they made us climb down.'

Velvet grips my hand. 'But that doesn't matter, right, Nin? Help is coming, isn't it?' She strains her neck to look behind me. 'Were they far behind you?'

I put my other hand over hers, feel the energy of our whisperling link. I can't lie to her, as much as I want to.

'No, Velvet. I don't think help is coming here. Something bad has happened to Lemon back there. We're going to have to do this ourselves.' I remove my hand and hold it back out to Flo. There is a crackle, like static. 'It's the only thing we've got. We have to try.'

The four of us – Maeve, Flo, Velvet and I – join hands.

'These are the bad ghosts,' I say. 'We have to reach out to the good ones.'

I don't tell them the real reason I want us to link. If we're not going to make it, which I don't think we are, I want to bring my sister here to be with me.

She's here.

But she's fading, and I realize with a gut punch that *this* will likely be the last time I ever see her, in this world, at least. I reach out to touch her face and my hand shimmers against her cheek like a pond skater on the surface of a pool.

'Hey, sis,' she says. 'Hey, girls.' She waves, and they wave back automatically, but then the terrible truth hits them.

'No!' cries Maeve, stricken.

'Oh Clemmy,' gasps Velvet. 'This can't be happening. You're the most alive person I know.'

'Stop it,' says Lemon. 'You know I hate a fuss.' I smile, in spite of the awfulness of it all. 'If we're

302

going to go out, we're going out with a bang,' she says, putting out her hand. 'Who's with me?'

'Me,' I say, covering her ghostly hand with mine. She looks at me and presses her other translucent hand to my face. I imagine her touch on my skin, but I can't feel anything, not really. It's like we're on different sides of a pane of glass.

'M-m-me.' Flo can barely get the word out, her doll-like features scrunched up in distress.

'Me too,' says Jessie, suddenly visible.

'Jessie!' we all say in unison.

'Jessie, does this work?' asks Maeve. 'We can't lose anyone else.'

'From here on in, we're unwritten, my friends.' Jessie flickers in and out of focus. 'I'm so sorry about Lemon, Nin.'

I can't answer.

'Let's do this for her,' says Velvet.

We link hands, and the effect is immediate; my chest fills with gentle light and I close my eyes, using the energy to push the dark clouds away. I know the others are doing the same and it's helping, but it isn't enough – these spirits, whatever they are, are furious. Angry souls, dead members of The Righteous perhaps, centuries of ratty, outraged, entitled men, poisoned and twisted by a vengeful obsession, even in death.

I open one eye. It isn't just the dead who are against us; the water is still rising, at least another foot in the last few minutes. There is no way out, even without the shrieking storm of spirits in our way.

A sob spools from my chest. I look up – there *must* be another exit – and spot the air pipes at the edge of the ceiling.

'Jessie! Look! It's like in our grotto. Those pipes must go somewhere!'

'But we can't get out through those, Nin – they're tiny!'

'No, but could we somehow use them to let people know we're down here?'

'But we've *tried* screaming and shouting,' says Maeve with a sob. 'The other girls have too, all the time they've been down here. No one ever heard them.' I think back to that fateful messaging. *All that screaming.* Not no one, exactly . . .

'Sing,' says Jessie. 'It's a different pitch.' She points to Velvet, who has her head on Flo's shoulder. 'Sing.'

'Sing?' echoes Velvet. 'Sing what?'

'Anything! Anything that will carry! Anything loud!'

'Concentrate!' yells Lemon. 'They're getting through!'

She's right; leaching, ragged spirits whip everywhere around us, tattered feelers scratching at our faces. They want to take us. They want to finish us. I look to Lemon, who looks behind her into the raging black then back to me, as if weighing up her options.

'Wait there,' she says, diving into the maelstrom.

'No!' I yell, but she's immediately engulfed, swallowed by the baying, snapping spirits. What does she think she's doing?

'Come *on*,' urges Jessie. 'Think of your loved ones. Reach to them. Strengthen us. And you, Velvet. Sing.'

Velvet sits upright and clears her throat. '*Pack up your troubles in your old kit bag,*' she begins, her voice quavering at first, then getting stronger. '*And smile, smile, smile.*' The storm rages around us. '*Don't let your joy and laughter hear the snag. Smile boys, that's the style.*'

I open an eye again. Amid the storm, all of us are mouthing the words. Velvet's rich, clear voice reverberates around the cave, bouncing from the walls. '*What's the use of worrying? It never was worth while.*' She grins. 'Everybody: join in, loud as you can!' And, one by one, we do, till we're all singing. All of us, together.

And then:

'Nin!' Shimmering like a million golden cobwebs, Lemon glides towards me through the storm. She looks like an angel.

And then Lemon gives me a very un-angelic grin.

*Something* floats in front of her. Confused, I rub at my eyes. And then I see. Somehow, my amazing, brave poltergeist of a sister has got her hands on the Book of Devona.

Not quite *in* her hands; from here, it looks like the Book of Devona floats through the air like a butterfly.

'Ready, Nin?' says Lemon.

*No*, I think, but she swings the book, readying to throw it.

'Your catch!'

The book loops high over the cave, swooping in a perfect arc. I pull my hands free and stretch out as far as I can, willing the book to connect to my fingers. When it hits my open palm I pull it quickly towards me.

I exhale in relief. Imagine if I'd dropped it!

'Keep singing, Velvet! Everyone!'

'*So, pack up your troubles in your old kit bag –*'

My hands pulse, blood rushing in my ears. I grip the book and pull it tight to my chest, hugging it fiercely. Below me, dark water churns and spits. I tuck my legs under me and hunch over the book, as if protecting a baby from a foe.

The book falls open, presumably on the page where Simons read from. My neck and shoulders clench as I remember how roughly he handled this precious volume. There's a special place in hell for people who crack the spine of a book. The swirling spirits dim the whisperling glow, but I shuffle until I can just about see what's written there. The hide-and-seek rhyme – *our* rhyme, my sister's and mine – is written on the page in Mam's hand. I'd recognize her handwriting anywhere.

I squint, scanning the text, checking for any mention of incantations or transference of power, and of course there is none.

'He made all that nonsense up! Every last bit of it.'

Rage at Simons and his 'brothers' burns in my chest, colliding with grief for my sister. That man, *those men*, those stupid, jealous, power-hungry men, meddling with things they don't understand – the notion that they might not know what they were doing never once entering their silly heads. No regard for any consequence. No consideration of the impact on others. I place a hand on each open page, and breathe in. The dark, congealed weight in my gut gently lifts, replaced by a bright, fierce light . . . and the sound of marching.

We sing, loudly, all of us:

'*And smile, smile, smile.*'

Breath catches in my throat. Tiny specks of light appear in the dark gloom of the cave, like pinpricks in a curtain letting through threadlike beams of sunlight. The ancient ones are here. And not only them . . .

'Gran?' I can't believe it. She's here, one of the jewels in this sparkling necklace of protection. And a noise, steady and sure and solid.

*Trudge, trudge, trudge. March, march, march.*

I crush the book to me, feel its strange heartbeat against mine.

And then I see them.

An army. Our boys. Thousands of them. Coming home.

They emerge through the walls, from the tunnels, from everywhere. *Did the book call them?* I imagine them peeling away from their living families, straightening up and snapping into formation as if on parade, drawing ghostly recruits to them like a magnet through iron filings as they marched through the city. Here, for one last battle.

They push through the tide of writhing, snapping ash and black, a khaki wall of bravery wanting to serve and protect, even in death. They don't have to fight; their presence here is enough.

'L-look,' whispers Jessie. 'I've never seen anything like this.'

Sparks of recognition ignite around the crypt. A young-looking cadet in a blue beret salutes Maeve and her mouth drops open. 'Emlyn?' she says. 'Cousin Emlyn?'

'Harry?'

'Dad?'

'Papa?'

In this small city, everyone has lost someone. Tears flow and we feel it, all of us, that feeling of love and pain and pride and strength.

'Good catch,' says one transparent, ghostly cadet, and I have a flicker of recognition, but can't place him. 'The book, I mean, when you caught it.' He grins, lopsidedly, and my tummy flips over. He's very young, and quite handsome. 'Sorry, by the way,' he adds, removing his beret to scratch his head. His fringe falls over one eye. 'I think it was my fault you fell into the canal. I made a wish, you see.'

*It can't be.* But it is, it's him, the ghost soldier who appeared at the side of the canal on the day of the rift. *Did I fall in, or did I swoon?* I dismiss the idea with a shake of my head. I also dismiss the idea of Lemon having a better time *there* than here, what with Ivy and now *him*.

'What did you wish for?' I ask, but his reply is swallowed in a deafening roar as the churning spirits rise from the floodwater like ragged, rotten kraken.

'S'cuse me, ma'am,' says the soldier. He turns his back on me, joining his comrades again to stand shoulder to shoulder. They push forward, little by little, herding the darkness back to wherever it is that it came from.

'It's working!' I whisper, huddling down with the girls to watch wide eyed as, sure enough, the storm settles and all we can hear is Velvet singing.

There's a splash and –

'Wilf?' My heart twists in my chest. Our friend is here, in his uniform, water up to his knees. Is he a ghost? I slide off the ledge into the freezing water. No, please no. Wait . . . is that Badger? Did The Righteous get him as they said they would? My sister, my friend and now my dog? My legs buckle, but an arm loops through mine and I'm dragged to my feet.

'It's me, Nin, it's me!'

'Wilf! You're alive?'

Wilf looks at me like I'm deranged. 'Of course I'm alive, you berk. Come on, we've got to get you out of here. They're pumping out the water but we haven't got long.' He looks around, astonished. 'Are we under the cathedral?' I nod, and Wilf sends word back. 'They'll get it opened up. Easier to get you out that way. Now, where's that dog? Badger? Where you at, boy?'

My little brown dog swims into the cave and Wilf scoops him up. He licks his face, delightedly.

'Oh my gosh, Badger, I thought you were a ghost!' I smush my cheek into his wet fur and ruffle his ears as he yips in excitement. 'There's a good boy, did you come and rescue us? What a clever boy . . . yes he is!' I look up at my friend, my gangly, brave, *alive* friend. 'How did you find us, Wilf? How did you get in here?'

'There's been searches goin' on fer hours.' He squints over my shoulder. 'If you're not injured,' he shouts, 'you should be safe to wade through.' The girls clamber gingerly down into the water. 'Orla got in touch with yer mams an' they made one holy hell of a fuss. The whole of Gloucester's been out there lookin' for you all.' He looks around and shakes his head in disbelief. 'Blimey O'Riley, there's yups of you!'

'You're not in trouble?'

He shakes his head. 'The Glosters came to the gaol an' spoke up for me. Some women from a protest group as well, though Lord knows how they knew about me.' He grins. 'Must be famous, ain't I? Anyway, th'army couldn't understand why I'd been arrested. They're lookin' after me.' He touches me on the cheek and then squeezes my nose and makes a *honk* noise. 'An' what's more – me dad's on the way back from France, Nin! He's injured, but alive.' He beams, joyous. 'We're gonna get the old boat cleaned right up, like she used to be.' He wipes his eyes with the back of his hand. 'Best not get too mushy though, eh? Not in front of the boys.' There's a shout behind him. 'Over here, lads!'

A dozen or so soldiers, some faces familiar from the pub, wade into the cave and immediately set about checking the girls over and piggy-backing them out. I ask Wilf how they got in and he tells me 'through a tunnel under the bookshop', which, after everything that's happened, seems totally obvious now, given how drawn I was to that shop. It must have been the missing girls I felt as I took shelter there. 'We could hear you through a tube by the front door,' he says. ''Twere the funniest thing. Owner had been away. Only got back this morning. Said they'd always wondered where the trap door went – turns out he hasn't had the shop long, see. I called him Mr Kip, but that ain't 'is name. "KIP's Bookshop". Short for "Knowledge Is Power." Ain't tha' a thing?'

I nod, flabbergasted. The times I've heard that phrase from Mam, Gran . . .

'Even had keys for it an' all.' He jangles a set of keys at me like a gaoler and points to the door they came in by, partly hidden from view. 'Like it was meant to be, ain't it?'

'You could hear us?'

Wilf nods. 'It was Velvet's singing that did it – at least it was what "pinpointed your location", according to the policeman. Made us all hush, he did. There's been reports of some sort of weird noises before, but it hadn't been taken serious, like.'

'Policeman?'

'Yeah, you've been giving him the runaround, apparently. He hasn't been trying to capture *you* though, Nin, he's been trying to find Velvet. His daughter.'

'Oh.' I feel a little foolish, realizing the man I thought was angry and frightening was actually stressed and frightened. 'But the posters . . . I saw him with a handful of posters, and I thought he'd taken them down?'

'He was taking *Velvet's* down. He said it weren't the right picture of 'er, no one would've recognized 'er. Then after the explosion at the pin factory –'

'Explosion?' I buckle, stricken. This is too much information. 'But Lemon is in there!'

'It's all right, Nin. We got 'er out.'

Grief punches my stomach. If Badger is here, then the mams are here. 'I have to tell the mams about Lemon,' I say numbly. 'How do I do that?'

Wilf shrugs. 'It's fine, Nin, they know. She looks a bit of a mess, like –'

I shove him backwards. 'A "bit of a mess"? A "bit of a mess"? How can you be so flippant! She's dead, Wilf. Dead!' I pummel my fists at his chest and he grips my wrists to stop me.

'No, she ain't, mate, I swear it. Not unless I've caught yer "whisperling-itis" and can see ghosts now. Yer sister is still very much alive.'

**45**

The soldiers lead the girls out one by one. They bring them up out of the cave, through the cathedral and out into the open arms of the city. Street lamps cast greeny-yellow moons on the ground and we blink and squint like moles coming out into the faint light. It's still raining, but not as heavily as before, the angry storm reduced now to a petulant drizzle. Someone immediately wraps a blanket round my shoulders and asks me my name, which they add to an ever-growing list.

'Oh my goodness.' I grip Wilf's arm in disbelief at what I'm seeing. 'Where did they all come from?' There are people, everywhere, stamping their feet and rubbing their hands together to keep warm. 'It's like the whole of Gloucester is here!'

The green outside the cathedral is especially busy; 'The "command centre",' explains Wilf. There are pockets of soldiers and rescue teams with ropes and torches. But there's civilians too, with blankets and towels and hot, sweet tea. Blythe Bumble, the clairvoyant, distributes biscuits, occasionally breaking bits off to feed an affectionate pet monkey on her shoulder. Wilf sees me looking. 'Found 'im half drowned in flood water, chained to a lamp post, she did. Cut the chain off 'im and they've been inseparable ever since.'

I'm flabbergasted. Not just about Blythe, but by *all* of this.

'Word spreads,' says Wilf with a shrug. 'The families of the missing girls kicked up merry hell an' between them and your mams . . . the whole city has pulled together.' He nods at a group of anxious-looking women craning their necks to see who is next out of the cave. 'Bin 'ere all night, some of 'em.'

Shrieks of recognition and joyful tears of reunion echo around the grounds, and then:

'Nin! Nin! Over here!'

'Lemon!'

She's sitting up on a stretcher, waiting to be loaded into the back of an ambulance. My sister, broken, but very much alive. Relief melts the bones in my legs and the mams run towards me, catching me as I'm about to buckle, and we hug, fast and fierce. The book, safely tucked under my damp top, pushes against my ribs. 'Oh Mam, thank God you're all right!' I pull her to me, feel the bones under her skin and I pull back. Under her eyes are smudges of grey. '*Are* you all right?'

She holds my cheeks with cold hands. 'I'm well enough, I promise. A bit tired, but much better.'

'I don't know what I was thinking,' says Bessie, hopping from foot to foot. I'm not sure if she's cold or agitated. 'On what shore is it acceptable parenting to send your child off into the city by herself?' She leans in to kiss me on the cheek. 'She was so poorly, Nin,' she whispers. 'And I was so frightened. But she's better, I give you my word.'

I nod, tears wobbling in my eyes as the mams move in for another hug, but I shake them off apologetically, desperate to get to my sister.

'I don't understand,' I say, falling to my knees beside her, tucking the scratchy brown blanket more tightly round her, touching her arms, legs, making sure she's all there. 'You were dead! I saw your ghost! How?' I ask, in wonderment. '*How?*'

I hold her face in my hands and she smiles, wincing in pain.

'Together forever, innit?' she manages before bursting into tears.

With the last girl freed, the rain stops and a strange quiet descends, like the silence of a battlefield after the last shot has been fired. They're still here, the ghost soldiers, milling around the cathedral grounds as if looking for a place to rest. We talk to some of the missing girls; they tell us how they worked out 'something weird' happened when they linked hands, and they tried to call for help, somehow. Perhaps that explains the odd visions the rest of us had, or the strange spooks I saw in the water. Something has been trying to help us, that's for certain, but there are so many uncertainties with the afterlife that we may never know who or what for sure.

Velvet is being hugged by her ecstatic father; Maeve holds hands and chatters excitedly with a woman who has very similar hair to hers. Flo, meanwhile, is deep in conversation with a very official-looking army gentleman. *I wonder what that's all about?*

Jessie is here, too, just about, flickering in and out of focus. Her voice is crackly, like a dusty gramophone record. I ask if she can tell me more details of what just happened, now that things are over. 'It's complicated,' she says. 'I'm not the first whisperling to be able to look back. There are a few of us, trying to stop bad things happening to all of us.' She pulls her sleeve up to show me the tiny eye and flame tattoo on her wrist, a symbol, she tells me, that modern whisperlings have adopted. I think it's even more thrilling than her nose-stud and the use of the word 'cool'. 'You know,' she says, 'it already feels different here.' She smiles, eyes shining with tears. 'Thank you, Nin. You don't yet know what you've done. But you will.'

'You said that *four* of us survived,' I say. 'Is that true?'

She shakes her head. 'I'm so sorry: I lied. In my reality, *none* of you survived. But how could I tell you that? I needed to see if you would be able to figure things out differently . . .' She trails off, shaking her head. 'The only thing I did was gather you together. Old newspaper cuttings helped us identify you. We had an idea that you and your sister were members of the Devona bloodline – your direct descendants

321

in my time are the spitting image of you both – and if we were to stand a chance against The Righteous then we needed to connect Devonas to their book. But you did all the rest.'

I nod. 'Talking of . . .' I say. We have already decided what to do next, in an exchange of quiet whispers. 'Shall we?' I reach out to 'hold' Jessie's hand. There's a staticky zap of energy.

Wordlessly, we all form a circle. All the creepers – or whisperlings or whatever you want to call us – surrounding everyone else gathered on the green. Around the soldiers, around the rescuers, around all of the good people from this city who have lost so very much. Around those who have not been able to say goodbye. Lemon insists her stretcher is carried over so she can be at my side, and for the stretcher bearers to step into the circle, too.

And then, something incredible happens. A number of *other* teenage girls, not just those rescued from the cave, step shyly forward. 'What are they doing?' Lemon whispers to me, but I know, *I know*. And, by the look on my sister's face, she knows it too.

'There are *more* of us?'

I grip her arm. *The rift did this*, I think, astonished. We've been so busy wondering *how* it happened – which I don't reckon we'll ever get to the bottom of – that we didn't consider what *else* it may have done! Suddenly, so much makes sense. One question in particular had been scratching at my brain like a branch at a window: what exactly did The Righteous think made a girl a whisperling? And how did they know who to single out? Girls who were *different* in some way? Girls who were *a bit much*?

I giggle involuntarily. The Righteous weren't *skilled* or *clever* in their selection of potential whisperlings. They were just *lucky*!

As my sister and I gaze at the growing circle of girls, wondering silently if perhaps *every teenage girl has the ability to be a whisperling*, a movement catches my eye: a small figure, scurrying mouse-like from shadow to shadow.

'Wait!' I shout. 'Lottie! Please come and join us,' I say, lifting my arm to gesture her into the circle. 'I promised, didn't I?'

She hesitates at first, but then tentatively makes her way over, hardly lifting her eyes. 'Thank you,' she says quietly, as she takes her place next to me in the ring. Suddenly she turns to me, stricken. 'But what if ma doesn't come?'

'She will,' I say, firmly. 'She's always been with you, Lottie.'

And then, safely tucked under my clothes, the book pulses against my heart. A wispy golden light washes over the cathedral, and fifty-seven members of the Creeper Gang – plus a few potential new recruits – link hands and set the world ablaze.

# EPILOGUE

Those that were there that night will never speak of it.

There will be no records, no articles written. Nothing public, at least. No one will tell of the eerie lights that looked like a giant had gathered the stars from the sky and thrown them over the cathedral. There will be no account of how – in that strange, magical circle – the fallen soldiers of Gloucester took one last leave of absence to bid their city goodbye. And not just soldiers: *anyone* in the circle who had lost someone had a moment of connection.

I looked away as Lottie touched her ma's face, smiling under her maid's cap, feather duster in hand, as always. Afterwards, Lottie was questioned by the police, but later released without charge. It was Simons who'd suggested Lottie rub the phosphorous unction over herself to make her 'shine' like a whisperling. '*They hope they can save my jaw,*' she wrote in her letter. The ghoul on Lottie's shoulder has gone, for now. '*Which I'm proper glad about, for he was getting heavier and heavier,*' she said. If it ever dares to return, Lottie's ma will dispatch it with a firm flick of her feather duster. She's staying now with Velvet and her family, an offer that made Lottie cry. Because although she hasn't seen much evidence of it in her short life, she's learning that most people are kind.

Wilf, too, had a reunion. The young soldier with the lopsided smile (who made me fall into the canal) was his friend from the front, the one who was accused of desertion and punished so terribly. I asked Wilf, later, if his friend had told him what he'd wished for. 'To come home, Nin. Like all of 'em.'

On 11 November 1918, the war finally ended. We would come to learn that a group of plucky Girl Guides acted as couriers, passing messages between those negotiating the peace. So if it hadn't been for Girl Guides, there might have been no signing of the Treaty of Versailles, and no end to the Great

War. Bravo, girls! We've no doubt Flo was involved, although she was sworn to secrecy.

We've made plans to meet up with our fellow creepers, because The Righteous, although weakened, will no doubt regroup, and we have to be ready. Detective Simons, however, won't be among them –

The papers say it's Gloucestershire's first case of 'Spontaneous human combustion', so Detective Simons did achieve a sort of fame in the end, if not his fortune. It was on account of the phosphorous . . . they call it the 'devil's element'. Simons flung it all over the place to make things glow and look spooky and everything went *boof*. Including him. That odious TR-inscribed signet ring of his was all that was left of him after the pin factory explosion. That, and the sausage-y little finger he wore it on. In his belongings, tucked inside a book on the black arts, they found a one-way ticket to America; he'd planned to set sail the day after the ritual. Little wonder he was so keen to get it done and collect his money from his 'brothers'; he was going to leave them behind to sort out his mess.

When Lemon and I finally got home to The Bargeman's in Oakdean-on-Severn, the mams pointed out our birthmarks: mine on my right shoulder, Lemon's on her left. Now they are full moons, not half. We aren't sure what it means, but we do know that *both* of us feel our powers growing and growing and growing. Since Lemon's brush with death, her powers are more than a match for mine. Annoyingly.

And where is the Book of Devona now? Well, that would be telling.

*We are the Creeper Gang.*
*We are whisperlings.*
*We are EVERYWHERE.*

*And by our deeds we are known.*

# ACKNOWLEDGEMENTS

Book two, whoo-hoo! We did it! I say 'we', because if it had just been 'me' I'd have collapsed in a heap and set fire to my laptop. So, on to the 'we' –

My Puffin family – thank you all for your patience, kindness and brilliance. Special mention to my lovely editor and pal Katie Sinfield. Katie, you have my word that my next first draft will feature zero bullet points/stream-of-consciousness bananas-ness. All budding writers, take heart – your first draft will never, ever be as bad as mine was for this book. But here we are!

Shreeta Shah for her endless good humour in the face of my last-minute tweaking (I'd have been so mad at me). To Kristina Kister for her incredible cover art and to Alice Todd and the design team for giving me a map! It's very humbling to have such talented people creating things for the words I wrote.

My agent, Megan Carroll, who guided me through book-two wobbles with humour, kindness and only the very mildest of threats. You rock.

To my female friends. Love you all. My writer pals, both irl and online. Amanda, Kate and Jane – literally couldn't do it without you. To each and every one of the #Debut22 OGs – you are all ace.

A heartfelt THANK YOU to the booksellers, bloggers, reviewers, librarians and teachers who tirelessly champion children's books. You are incredible. And Rosie Hudson. You are a joy. Thank you.

To established children's authors who are so generous with their support. Emma Carrol deserves a special mention.

My lovely parents who have turned bookseller bothering into an art form. Love you, Mum and Dad.

Ollie, my son, here I am, mentioning you again – will you read it now?

To Steve, for continually bossing his mission as The World's Best Husband™.

To the City of Gloucester, for its architecture, history and people, and to 'The Glorious Glosters' for giving the book its motto:

By our deeds we are known.

Love,
H xx